BROTHER GUN

"Who hired you, Freddie? The three of you together didn't have enough brains to fill the pocket watch of a midget," Lassiter said in disgust.

"Shoulda killed you right off . . . way to do it . . . I told him that when he hired us, but he didn't want the law . . ."

"Let me hear a name. Who the hell hired you?"

"You . . . you'll find out. Them's our kinfolk you killed . . ."

Lassiter had had enough. He leveled his gun at Freddie's head. "I asked a name. I want it."

Freddie's breathing had eased, but his lips were still white with pain. He stared at the gun pointed at his left eye and said, "Ed. Ed Covey."

Lassiter:

Brother Gun

Jack Slade

LEISURE BOOKS

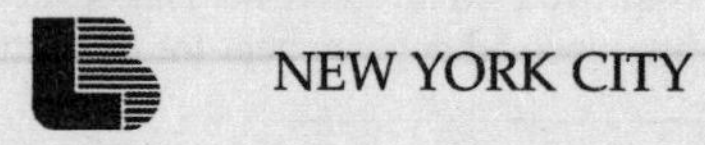

NEW YORK CITY

A LEISURE BOOK®

August 2009

Published by

Dorchester Publishing Co., Inc.
200 Madison Avenue
New York, NY 10016

ISBN 10: 0-8439-6238-0
ISBN 13: 978-0-8439-6238-3
E-ISBN: 978-1-4285-0716-6

Printed in the United States of America.

10 9 8 7 6 5 4 3 2 1

LASSITER:
Brother Gun

Chapter One

Sweat stung Lassiter's eyes as he strained to spot any movement of the two men who intended to kill him. They were at opposite ends of the clearing that was part junkyard, part corral. The Monagals, father and son, were hidden well; Bert, the old man, was crouched behind a stack of beer barrels. His lanky son, Con, with the instincts of a stepped-on rattlesnake, was hunched behind a partially dismantled freight wagon tipped on its side. A pile of used bricks was a barricade for Lassiter.

A tense whisper reached Lassiter from a window of the trading post a dozen feet behind him. "Lassiter, I did not know they were out there." It was Miguel Aleman, owner of the place.

"Not your fault, Miguel. Stay out of it."

"The gate. It should not have been left open. That is how they got in." Miguel spoke in Spanish, his voice anguished. "I will have to speak to Elnora about such carelessness."

Speak to her about more than that, old friend, Lassiter felt like saying.

"The feud ends today, Lassiter," Bert Monagal screeched, "with you *dead*!"

"You haven't got a chance, Bert," Lassiter bluffed.

Bert Monagal laughed. "Ain't nobody inside but the old Mex. We seen his wife ridin' out west an hour ago . . ."

Con added his assessment of Elnora Aleman. "I got

me an itch just thinkin' about that filly," he tittered from behind the upended wagon.

"An' that damn son of Miguel's is likely off drunk somewheres," Bert finished. "So you got nobody to back you up, Lassiter."

"In all these years I never needed anybody to back me up when it came to you Monagals!" Lassiter called out.

"This is the end of it, Lassiter."

"Bert, you're a windy old son-of-a-bitch!" Lassiter cocked his .44, cursing himself that he had left his Winchester inside.

"Ain't I, though." Bert Monagal chuckled. "We heard you hole up here ever once in a while. Wa'al after all this time we got patience when it comes to you. Damn if we don't see you ride in last evenin'. But the place is fulla people. So we waits. An damn if that young Senora Aleman don't go off an' leave the gate open for us. All we had to do was either go in an' get you. Or stay out here till you come to us. Which you done."

"Stand up where I can see you, Bert. Let's talk . . ."

"You get in bed with Miguel's purty young wife last night, Lassiter?"

"Shut your goddamn mouth, Bert!"

"If you didn't bed her last night, you'll never have another chance."

Lassiter squirmed. Last night he'd had the idea. "You're talking about another man's wife!" he yelled back at Bert Monagal.

"Ol' fool like Miguel, takin' hisself a young filly!" A spate of hysterical laughter burst from Bert Monagal. Lassiter tensed, waiting for one of them to show a face, a hand, or even a finger.

He swore at himself for walking into the trap. Of all people on this warming mid-morning he hadn't expected the Monagals, although he had heard they were running a few head of cattle somewhere in the territory. He had come outside, after spending the night at the trading post, with other things on his mind. There had been some trouble in El Paso and he wanted to make sure none of those involved had trailed him here. Instead, he had found the last of the Monagals, ready to settle an old feud.

And now the pair thought they had him whipsawed behind the two-story trading post known across the frontier as Aleman's Barn. There was a store crammed with merchandise, then a dining room with a few tables and next to it a small saloon. Living quarters were on the second floor with two rooms for overnight guests. Lassiter had known Miguel's first wife and their eldest son, Refugio. Now only Miguel and his son Juanito were alive.

Lassiter turned his head cautiously behind the pile of bricks to stare up at the second floor windows, almost narrow enough for rifle ports, a reminder of days when some of the great Apache chiefs resented skins paler than their own. The Monagals, dead shots, would blow Miguel right out of his own window if he foolishly showed himself. Lassiter had intended to lay over here for a month until the El Paso business cooled down. If the Monagals had their way he would be buried here.

They were taunting him again. Lassiter knew there was little chance of interruption this early in the day. Nearby ranches were busy with the final stages of roundup and travelers rarely stopped by until later in the day.

And neither Juanito nor his father's young bride were present, having ridden away in different directions an hour or so earlier. Lassiter smelled rendezvous.

Pity for Miguel deepened. A man builds a prosperous business, then trades his good sense for a sensuous bundle of red-gold hair and hot eyes.

Bert Monagal yelled impatiently, "Throw down your gun an' step out where we can see you!"

"I'm in no mood for humor, Bert!" Lassiter's mouth tasted like a sheepherder's boot. His head pounded. He looked again at the open gate that Elnora had left open. She should have known by now that a rider leaving by the gate was supposed to swing it shut so that a bar, weighted with a sack of sand, would lock in place. If anyone wanted to get to the yard or corrals, they had to enter from the trading post. It was Miguel Aleman's way of discouraging horse thieves.

Elnora Aleman had disrupted his visit from the first. To find Miguel with a brand new wife had been a shock.

After a fast trip from El Paso, Lassiter drank too much. He talked too much. He told Miguel, "Why didn't you let the woman stay around till you got your fill? Why'd you go and marry her . . ."

She overheard his remark.

Miguel Aleman had risen to his toes, which made him slightly over five feet tall, and tried to hit Lassiter in the face. Lassiter apologized. Drunk or not, he shouldn't have butted into another man's business. Especially an old friend like Miguel.

Lassiter's eyes strained between the two unseen targets across the junk-filled yard. Through the open gate in the stockade could be seen distant hills, then a barrier of mountains, their peaks lost in banks of scudding clouds.

"Only reason I ain't killin' you right off," Bert Monagal's old voice squeaked from behind the barricade of whiskey bottles. "is 'cause I want you up close. For what you done to our kin . . ."

"When I killed Monagals, it was to save my own neck!"

Bert Monagal's voice was beginning to crack from tension; it gave Lassiter faint hope. "You gonna throw out that gun, Lassiter? Or will me an' Con cut you in half?"

"You're too old for this game, Bert! You're not using your head . . ."

"We got you boxed!" Bert Monagal countered. "That's usin' my head!"

"Look at it this way. You may get me, Bert. But I'll kill your boy. I'll put five bullets right through the bed of that wagon he's hiding behind. Five shots right into Con."

"Lassiter is spittin' a big wind, Pa," Con called to his father, but sounding a little nervous. "He can't even see me!"

"I've had no quarrel with most of you Monagals, but for five years you've been hell bent to kill me!" Lassiter shouted. "Now you and your boy clear out while you've got a chance!"

"After we work you over with our knives, we'll do the same with your greaser friend inside!" Bert countered.

Lassiter winced, hoping Miguel hadn't heard the insult. For sure, there was no one else inside to hear it. Always there had been a man and wife and a barkeeper and sometimes a handy man to help out. But they had left when Miguel took on a new wife.

"Bert, you listen close!" Lassiter called. "I'm giving you a chance to get out."

"You killed our kinfolks, Lassiter! Nothin' else counts!"

"Old man, you even remember what started this goddamn feud?"

Silence, while some of the mules in the corral beyond the junkyard started to bray. "Was somethin' to do with Uncle Tim, as I recollect," Bert Monagal said tentatively. "But we was off south when it happened an' I ain't sure . . ."

"It wasn't Tim Monagal. It was Ham. Christ, he was drunk and he owed me money and he reached for his wallet with one hand and two-shot derringer with the other. To keep my liver from being splattered, I had to kill him."

"Ham owed you money? Hell, I never heard that part of it . . ."

"You heard it now, Bert. Now you and Con get the hell out of here!" Lassiter made his voice tough; he knew Bert was getting edgy and tired. "Either that or Con will never leave. That's your last son, Bert. You'll be alive, sure. And I'll be dead. But so will your son. You'll be a lonely old man."

"Don't listen to him, Pa!" Con shouted from behind the wagon. "You say the word, I'll blow off his head."

"Come to think of it, son, I doubt you can even see his head," Bert said. He gave a deep sigh that Lassiter could hear across the yard. "Reckon Lassiter means what he says, Con. Turns me cold thinkin' that you might end up dead in here."

"But, Pa . . ."

"You heard me, Con," the snap back in the old voice. "Next time we won't try an' get him alive so's we can work on him with our knives. We'll blow out the back of his head."

"That's where I've got another set of eyes, Bert," Lassiter said coldly. "I can look both ways at once."

"Damn if sometimes I don't believe you can at that. Lassiter, you lettin' us ride out like you said?"

"Just don't try tricks. I'm in no mood for any."

And just when Lassiter thought he might have the thing settled, for now at least, without Miguel getting his place shot up, or Miguel himself, for that matter, or any customer with his family in tow who happened to wander in at the wrong moment. Not that Lassiter had much regard for human life, other than women and children. And Miguel . . . he did owe something to Miguel because of Refugio.

Just when he smelled victory, it all turned sour.

Bert Monagal seemed to be making up his mind. He stirred, showing the crown of an old hat. Then a horse at a canter intruded on the tense silence. Lassiter risked moving his head around the bulwark of bricks; the horse sounds were coming from the flats, not the road. He hoped no one foolishly accepted the invitation of the open gate instead of going around front as was customary. He prayed it wouldn't be that surly Juanito, perhaps fired up even this early in the day on forty rod. Miguel had already lost one son, Refugio. He didn't deserve to lose a second. Even if this one was worthless. At least in Lassiter's estimation.

It wasn't Juanito on the horse. It was his new stepmother, Elnora. Lassiter could see the slim woman in shirt and Levis mounted on a bay, speeding up now. Braids of red-gold hair bounced across the front of a striped shirt as if calling attention to her breasts. Lassiter swore under his breath. She was heading straight for the open gate she had left open. He shouted a warning.

"Senora Aleman! *Stay back!*"

Either she failed to understand or in her female

contrariness, because of what she had overheard him say about her last night, chose to ignore the warning. She slowed her horse and fast-walked it into the yard. Neither of the Monagals moved.

"Mr. Lassiter," she said loudly in mock surprise, "you're still here. I was so hoping you'd be gone by the time I returned . . ."

He saw a flash of white teeth, the lively blue eyes. She was supposed to be part Mexican, according to Miguel. Lassiter doubted it. But you couldn't always tell about that. Miguel's son Juanito was even fairer than Senora Aleman, now swinging her horse toward, of all places, the upended wagon.

"Spur that horse!" Lassiter yelled. He sprang up from behind the pile of bricks. Sight of his drawn .44 caused her jaw to drop. He had a feeling it wasn't the first naked gun her kind had seen. But his reaction and her squeal of fear, he realized a moment later, was caused by the male arm suddenly clamped around her waist. Con Monagal pulled her backward out of the saddle, on the far side of the bay horse. The animal reared, snorting, and spun away, stirrups flapping.

Above her scream sounded Con Monagal's gleeful cry of triumph. "Pa, we got the son-of-a-bitch now! He won't dare shoot for fear of hittin' the woman . . ."

Just one fleeting glimpse Lassiter had of Con's long face as he started to haul the terrified woman back against his chest so as to use her body as a shield. He saw the long glinting barrel of Con's gun. Saw it slide between the neck of the woman and a braid of hair that had fallen forward. She was arched against him, off balance. Her eyes no longer filled with mischief he thought he had detected at their first meeting last evening. Now they were bright with fear, the moist lips formed an oval for an incipient scream.

Lassiter bounded aside. Con tried to follow him with the gun, then abruptly changed tactics; to ran the snout of his weapon against Elnora Aleman's ribs. But Lassiter's gunhammer dropped an eyewink sooner. In the roar and belch of smoke and cordite, part of Con Monagal's jaw disintegrated. Con started to spin around. Lassiter's second shot struck the heavy bone arch above the right eye. It made a neater but deadlier wound than the first. Con's knees caved.

Lassiter had started to wheel, ready to finish off the elder Monagal. Just as he was leveling his gun there was a cannon roar at his back. He saw Bert Monagal's stringy old frame leap into the air, as if jerked three feet off the ground by a skyhook. Lassiter remembered as a boy, seeing a rabbit in flight struck by the loads from a double-barreled shotgun. Monagal's dirty white shirt seemed indented with small black specks, like thrown pepper. Almost instantly they reddened. As he came crashing down, a redness shot up into his mouth and over the chin.

Miguel Aleman came at a trot from a rear door of his trading post, shotgun in his right hand. Wisps of smoke trailed from twin barrels.

The diminutive dark man flashed his teeth at Lassiter as he ran toward the terrified Elnora. "At last, my friend, you are in my debt!" he shouted. "I saved your life!"

Lassiter opened his mouth to correct the old Mexican, then shrugged it off. Miguel led his sobbing wife inside. Specks of flesh and bits of jawbone made a grisly pattern on one sleeve of her shirt.

Lassiter felt let down. The end of a senseless feud, he thought. Dead and buried, this business of Monagals.

He didn't know it then, but a new and even deadlier feud was in the making. . . .

Chapter Two

As long as there had been no outside witnesses to the double killing, Lassiter felt it best that such scum were better off buried anonymously in some lonely grave. Better than having a sheriff ask pointed questions. Lassiter had no wish to spend time in another jail. The Monagals were unmarried and wouldn't be missed; the best cow thieves uncaught in the territory, was how some people referred to the father and son.

After explaining the situation to Miguel and red-eyed Elnora, Lassiter drove off with the bodies in a wagon, the Monagal horses tied on behind. Deep in the hills he turned the horses loose, after first unsaddling them. Then he dug two graves.

Lassiter nursed his third whiskey in Miguel's small saloon. The only customers were some miners who had stopped off on their way to the Ober Hills. Miguel waited on them.

Elnora had washed her face and put on a blue dress. Her hair was pinned back. "I want to thank you, Lassiter," she said, coming to his end of the bar. "You saved my life, I'm sure of that."

"A damned lucky shot is all."

Her lips curled in a smile of disbelief. "Good marksmanship, you mean. We got off to a bad start last night. I'm sorry if I seemed to take a dislike to you. I know you did to me."

The miners, roughly dressed men, had turned to stare at Elnora. Miguel hurried up to her, his small face puckered. He drew her aside and spoke sharply in a low voice. She shrugged and walked away.

Lassiter followed her into the empty dining room. "You and Miguel arguing already?"

"He doesn't like me to be downstairs," she said with a tight smile. "People might look at me."

"You supposed to stay upstairs all day?"

"And do needlepoint, I guess. I'm too restless for that."

He took a chair at one of the empty tables. "Yeah, I can see it in your eyes, for sure." She didn't like his grin.

"Don't get smart, Lassiter. I owe you my life, maybe, but it doesn't give you the right to demean me."

"Fancy word."

"And don't add to it by saying fancy woman. If you do, I'll crack you across the mouth." She threatened with her backhand, staring defiantly up into his face. Poor Miguel at his age had acquired a fireball. Lassiter decided to apologize.

"You speak well. It surprised me is all."

She accepted that. "Miguel thinks he can carry the load himself. He needs me."

"How about that big son of his?" Lassiter asked quietly, wondering if he could read anything in her face.

"Juanito is . . . well, hard to handle. Miguel should let me help keep the accounts straight, wait on customers . . ."

And decorate the place for the male customers, Lassiter thought. Decorate it very well indeed with her delicate nose, high forehead, good breasts and enticing swell of hips. If she wasn't Miguel's wife . . . Reluctantly he pushed the idea aside.

"Why not hire somebody to help out there?" he suggested.

"Not easy to do . . . under the circumstances."

"What circumstances? Miguel's always been able to hire people."

"The Millers quit on us and took the handy man and the bartender with them. I must help out, but Miguel is stubborn."

"Why'd the Millers quit?"

Her smile was strained. "Because it's immoral for a man Miguel's age to have a young wife. Simple as that. Ada Miller yelled Bible passages at me until I lost my temper and told her to shut up." She leaned both hands on the table, looking at him. "Maybe you can convince Miguel that I must do my part around here. He'll listen to you."

"I don't know about that."

"He says you and his son Refugio were great friends."

"Yeah." Lassiter sipped from his glass, feeling uncomfortable as he always did whenever reminded of their final venture. A deal in wet cattle. A disaster. Poor planning and Lassiter blamed himself.

"Miguel says Refugio had an . . . accident. And was killed."

Lassiter was on his guard, giving the smooth, slightly tanned face with the bright eyes a closer look. Did such a fetching female, so out of place in this remote trading post, by any chance have a Pinkerton badge pinned to her lacy underwear?

She changed the subject to the live son. "Miguel wishes you could be closer to Juanito. Juanito needs guidance."

"Was he my kid he'd straighten up. Or I'd give him the toe of my boot."

"But Juanito is so big and Miguel so . . . so small."

"Yeah, even shorter than you, so I noticed."

She bristled. "It makes not one damn bit of difference to me. Get that through your head, Lassiter." Here was one touchy female.

"I like you better when you talk that way." He gave her a malicious grin. "Instead of using words like demean."

The miners drank up and departed. Miguel sank wearily to a chair at Lassiter's table. "A strange day. Only a little past noon and two men dead and most of the cold beer is gone. I'll have to fetch more . . ."

"Juanito ought to be here to help you," Lassiter cut in angrily. He wondered if the old man had seen his son ride east that morning, shortly before Elnora had ridden west. Lassiter had searched for signs of guilt on Elnora's face whenever Juanito's name came up. But he had found none.

"Juanito," Miguel sighed. Dark eyes in the small wrinkled face were probing. A shock of gray-black hair was looped across his forehead. "It is Senor Dios blessing me this day, Lassiter."

"God had nothing to do with this day." Lassiter was on guard, sensing Miguel was leading up to something he wouldn't like to hear. Elnora had gone upstairs.

Miguel Aleman spoke haltingly. "I always feel you are . . . like one of my own family. Poor Refugio . . . he looked on you as a brother. I . . . I wish you could look on Juanito as *your* brother."

Lassiter squirmed in his chair. "Refugio was more my own age. We had things in common."

"I know what things," Miguel said with a weary smile. "No, do not be offended." He was speaking in Spanish, feeling more comfortable in that language. "I have also done things . . . outside the law." Miguel looked pained for a moment, then shook his head.

"I knew Refugio's weaknesses. He used to worry his mother. I know that you and he . . . had interests in Chihuahua cattle, among other things. But I never said anything. And because he is dead, there is no blame attached to you."

Lassiter didn't say anything; he drank, waiting.

Miguel reached across the table and gripped Lassiter by a wrist. "Now after today at last you are in my debt."

"Me in your debt?" The whiskey suddenly tasted bitter.

"I saved your life," Miguel reminded soberly.

Again Lassiter was on the verge of setting the old Mexican straight on that point. But being reminded of Refugio decided him to humor his friend. With a wild young son and a young wife who, in Lassiter's worldly judgment, could be equally wild, Miguel did need humoring. "My friend, you saved my life with that shotgun."

Miguel brightened. "To repay me, I would like you to be blood brother to Juanito."

Lassiter looked at him. A matter of blood was not to be taken lightly by a man like Miguel, who had in his veins the fierce pride of the Spaniard, the honor of the Indian.

"Miguel, listen to me . . ." Then the image of the laughing, irresponsible Refugio Aleman filled his mind. The very dead Refugio, because Lassiter took the wrong escape route down an alley. Lassiter making it to the desert and safety, Refugio cut down by weapons in the hands of rustlers who objected to being robbed of their plunder.

"It would mean so much to me," Miguel implored. "You are a man of strength. If something should happen to me, I could rest easier if I knew you looked out for Juanito."

"And if something happens to you, who looks after your bride? Do I become blood brother to her?"

Miguel's lips whitened. "You jest, and it is . . ."

"Miguel, for Chrissakes, you only made trouble for yourself by taking a wife who is practically the same age as your son." Lassiter banged a fist on the table. "Hell, I should keep my mouth shut . . ."

"You do not understand about Elnora . . ."

"Sorry I even mentioned her." Lassiter's smile was tight. "I'll be blood brother to Juanito. If it's so important to you."

Miguel looked relieved. "It is important." Then he spoke of Elnora again, but Lassiter interrupted.

"It's none of my business. Last night I was fairly drunk and shouldn't have said what I did. Today I'm cold sober and I've got even less excuse."

"A terrible thing for a woman to be alone out here. She had a husband and he was killed near Santa Fe. She drifted down this way. She was hungry, despondent . . ." Miguel's voice began to shake. "All that I can say is that a drifter, a young woman, deserves some honor in life. That I have given her by making her my wife."

Lassiter braced himself, expecting tears to spill from the black eyes framed by deep sun wrinkles. He had no wish to see this proud old Mexican weep; it would embarrass them both. "Where the hell is Juanito?" Lassiter said with false heartiness, "so we can get this ritual over with."

Miguel explained that Juanito had ridden out in the early morning, which Lassiter already knew. It had been shortly before Elnora had also left the compound.

Miguel seemed to read his thoughts. "Do not think things, old friend. Juanito rode in one direction, Elnora in another. My son maybe have inherited wild blood, but he has honor."

"Inherited no wild blood from you, Miguel," said Lassiter trying to cover it up. "I remember his mother, Luz. A fine and gentle lady. Refugio was the only one with wild blood."

"You young scoundrels." Miguel's smile was weak.

"I don't think Juanito is wild . . . well, it's different than with Refugio. With Juanito it's . . ." Lassiter groped for the right words; other things he had put badly. "It's as if something is bothering him. Maybe it's because he's so tall and the rest of the family so short. And he's light-skinned where you're dark. Maybe he doesn't *feel* Mexican . . ." Lassiter noticed a pallor begin to spread across the small dark features. "Miguel, are you sick . . . ?"

"No . . . no, it is nothing. I . . . I think the bloodletting upset me more than I thought."

When Juanito had not returned by late afternoon, Miguel said he had probably gone north to Kendall Springs where he often spent the night. Aleman's Barn was the only trading post between the settlement at Kendall Springs, twenty miles north, and the Santa Cruz Valley to the south. Miguel had built a profitable business because he controlled the only source of supply for many miles. But the whole place to Lassiter looked as if it might be disintegrating. A new wife, a no-good son. Lassiter clenched his teeth.

Lassiter took a bath that afternoon, carrying tub and hot water up to his room. He was naked in the wooden tub before realizing he had forgotten soap. He heard someone moving around in an adjoining room. "Miguel . . . hey, Miguel . . ."

"What is it, Lassiter?" Elnora's voice came through the closed door. "Miguel's downstairs."

Lassiter thought of telling her to forget it, then for pure devilment said, "I need soap. The door's unlocked."

She stepped away from the door, returning in a few moments. She opened the door a crack. He could see her foot, a curved ankle, a lacy hem of underskirt. She sent something sliding across the floor then closed the door with a bang. Grinning, he climbed out of the tub and retrieved the soap. It was in a jar. It was strongly scented. *Her* soap.

"I'll smell like a Bourbon Street whore."

He and Miguel were in the small dining room, eating the supper Elnora had cooked for them, when some teamsters pulled their rigs in behind the trading post. Miguel left the table to serve them whiskey. They were big, boisterous, dusty and weary after a long haul over the mountains. They emptied one bottle quickly and called for another. Elnora said she'd serve them; Miguel could finish his meal. Miguel gave a quick shake of his head.

After Miguel had gone to take care of his customers, Elnora came out of the kitchen with a coffee pot. She refilled Lassiter's cup. "Why don't you sit down and eat?" Lassiter asked.

"I'm not hungry." Eyes that had seemed so lively, now were troubled. She barely looked at him in the lamplight. She seemed to have gone out of her way to make herself unattractive. She wore a loose-fitting brown dress and had done her hair up severely in a bun. He had the feeling that she and Miguel had quarreled again.

When Elnora returned to the kitchen, her shoes padding lightly on the plank floor, he noticed that the men had left the bar and were gathered in the archway leading to the dining room. They nudged one another. A big black-whiskered man gave a booming laugh.

"Tell the gal to step out here," he said to Lassiter. The man had a missing front tooth. His eyes, small and reddened from road dust and whisky, darted to the kitchen where Elnora stirred something in a kettle.

"Go back to your drinking," Lassiter said coldly.

The man glared at Lassiter who sat quietly at a table. "You got wax in your ears, mister? I said tell her to step out where we can have a good look at her."

One of the men laughed nervously. "Better go easy, Woody."

Woody started for the kitchen, slouching along on thick legs. Lassiter got to his feet. "That's far enough."

Woody slid to a halt, teetering slightly in his inebriation. He started to say something, but one of the men from the saloon pushed through the others packed in the archway. He saw Lassiter, saw the holstered .44.

"Let it go, Woody, let it go." Then he turned a pale worried face to Lassiter. "He was only funnin'. Meant no harm. Come on, Woody . . . *Woody!*"

"I been too long without a woman, damnit . . ."

Lassiter interrupted Woody. "She happens to be Miguel Aleman's wife!"

The men looked surprised. "Miguel . . . married?" said the pale-faced man in the doorway. "We never knowed he had a new wife."

"Time he let everybody know," Lassiter snapped.

Woody leveled a forefinger. "You're a goddamn liar!" he bellowed. "She gimme the eye, I know she did an' she ain't nobody's wife. Not her kind . . ."

Woody lunged for the doorway. Elnora backed up to the stove. Lassiter caught him before he could get into the kitchen. Woody started to yell something. The tail end of Woody's sentence ended in a great poof of breath that escaped the cavernous mouth; it burst open when Lassiter's fist slammed into the solar plexus. Woody, gasping, made a faltering pass at a yellowed ivory gun butt. Lassiter threw a right. It crashed into the jaw, turning the head at a ludicrous angle. As if Woody had found something of interest on the ceiling while at the same time trying to dig a morsel from between his teeth with a tongue tip. Whatever momentarily held him erect came suddenly apart. He crashed jarringly.

Miguel appeared with his lethal weapon of that morning. The face of every teamster and swamper blanched at sight of the shotgun, hammers eared back.

Lassiter rubbed his knuckles. "Pass the word," he snarled at them, "that Senora Aleman is a *lady!*"

Angrily he jacked cartridges from the ivory-butted gun Woody had dropped. He flung them into a spittoon. Lassiter felt on edge. In one day he had killed two men, knocked another one down. He handed the empty weapon to one of the men.

"You tell Woody if he even loads this gun before you pull out in the morning, I'll blow off his head."

They were impressed. "Nobody ever knocked Woody down before, drunk or sober," one of them said in an awed voice.

They were just ordinary men in a very tough game, drinking too much when they had the chance, and some of them, as in Woody's case, expecting too much. After Woody had been half-carried at a stumbling walk out back to the wagons, Elnora spoke.

"Lassiter, you shouldn't have butted in. It could have ended in a tragedy."

"Woody was about to take what he wanted."

From a dress pocket she removed a .32 with pearl grips. "I don't think so."

Miguel looked at the weapon in surprise, then at Lassiter. "Tell her she should stay upstairs when men are here . . ."

"I don't think I could tell her much of anything." Lassiter's gaze locked with Elnora's blue eyes.

Cowhands from one of the nearby ranches came tramping in, spurs rattling. They had finished roundup earlier than most outfits.

Miguel decided to make a speech. He gestured at Elnora who was cleaning off a table. "That is Senora Aleman, my wife. Treat her as such or you are not welcome here."

He forgot himself and spoke in Spanish, which some did not understand. He said it again, this time in English.

Some of the cowhands were already aware that Miguel had married again. Those who didn't, said, "Howdy, ma'am," and that was that.

Miguel waited on evening trade in the bar. Elnora was doing the evening dishes. Lassiter ground his teeth, wishing Juanito would walk in. Lassiter felt like giving him a sample of what he had given Woody earlier in the evening, for letting his father and stepmother do all the work. There was no damned excuse for such indolence.

Lassiter picked up a flour sack dishtowel and started in on the stack of dishes. Elnora eyed him. "Surprised you'd lower yourself to woman's work," she said crisply.

"You better go upstairs and stay like Miguel wants you to."

"You know very well I won't."

"Yeah. I guess some people would call it spunk."

"Independence," she snapped.

From the barroom came a murmur of voices, clink of glasses, laughter, chime of spurs when men shifted their feet. Lassiter dried another dish. He wondered if he could get Elnora angry enough to let her slip her real reason for marrying Miguel. Hoping he'd die and she'd inherit a wife's share? What else?

"You married Miguel for better or worse," he jibed, "and promised to obey."

"I married him to be his partner in this . . ." She waved a dripping hand at the four walls, "venture."

"You've had other activities in your short life," he drawled.

"Your innuendos I can do without."

"Another one of your fancy words, like demean. You talk like a college professor I used to play poker with."

"I never had much schooling, if that's what you're hinting at. But I love to read. And I listen to conversations . . . I pick up things."

He almost commented on that, then decided to let it alone. "Self-education," he muttered. "For some people it's the best way, I guess."

"For me it was the only way." She thrust a wet plate into his hand; he toweled it dry. "It's one thing I admire about Juanito," she continued.

"Tell me." Qualities as a lover? Lassiter wondered.

"Juanito attended a few classes up at Kendall Springs, so he told me. But mostly he's read books. Everything he can get his hands on."

"Yeah, everything he can get his hands on," he said, looking her over.

"A lot of people would be surprised to find a full set of Shakespeare in his room."

"You've been in his room . . . to look it over?"

"An old set to be sure, rain-marked and some of the pages are missing. He bought it off a peddler who came through here. And yes, I got your snide remark. I only went into his room to straighten it up. He was not there at the time. You satisfied, Mr. Lassiter?"

She was beginning to rub him raw. He looked down at her straight back, seeing the curve of hip, the fetching backside. "There are times I feel like taking the flat of my hand to your . . ."

"I'll put a bullet in you, Lassiter!"

"I've been threatened by other females. One night I woke up half-drunk, without a stitch on. And my love of the evening had a dagger at my throat. The point was pricking the skin so that I felt my own blood."

"A pity she didn't finish the job. I suppose with your great charm you talked her out of murdering you."

"Just the way it happened."

"You are without doubt the most conceited man I ever met."

"In spite of myself, I do like your fire."

"Well, I don't like yours."

"I'd be tempted to sample that fire of yours . . ." And when she whirled on him, he held up a warning hand. "But I never would. Because Miguel's my friend. And you're his wife."

"Yes, I am." She stared down at the dishwater.

"Your great love was that dead husband of yours, I suppose."

"So Miguel told you I was married before."

"Mentioned it."

"Well, I hated that husband. I was married when I was thirteen. Thank God I don't seem to have the capacity for bearing children. I'd hate to think of his brood turned loose on the world."

"Miguel your great love?"

"I respect him. Honor him as a man."

"He know it's respect, not love?"

"We talked it over before we married. I thought it only honest."

"And still he married you?"

"He felt sorry for me. And . . . and . . . I don't know why, but sometimes I have a feeling he did it to ease his conscience.

Lassiter looked at the smooth cheek, the curve of lips. "Ease his conscience about what?" he asked skeptically.

"I would never ask. It's none of my business. Or yours."

When the last cowboy was gone, Miguel closed up. Lassiter helped him blow out some of the lamps, adjust low wicks for night lights on others. From a narrow side window of his second floor room Lassiter could look down at the teamsters. A campfire glowed on the big rigs. Their bull teams had settled down near hay furnished by Miguel.

He thought of Woody camped with the other teamsters who just might not heed the warning Lassiter had passed along. To be on the safe side, Lassiter placed his Winchester on the floor beside his bed, within easy reach. He put his .44 under the pillow.

He thought of Juanito, staying away all night, shirking his duty. Lassiter had asked Miguel if Juanito had a girl up at Kendall Springs. But Miguel was evasive.

The teamsters pulled out at first light. Lassiter stood with arms folded watching them hitch up. Woody, his jaw swollen, yelled at his swamper but was careful not to look directly at Lassiter.

By mid-morning Juanito had not returned, but a dark-haired girl, who appeared with five riders, caught Lassiter's attention. He was curious about the stunning young lady who walked into the store. He saw her flipping impatiently through a catalogue.

Miguel came in from the bar, saw her there and lost color. "*You,*" he said under his breath.

The young woman lifted her finely-molded chin. "I want to talk about Juanito," she said imperiously.

Chapter Three

Miguel seemed on edge; he wasn't the only one. Lassiter was impatient for Juanito's return so he could fulfill his promise to Miguel and be on his way. Aleman's Barn was beginning to get on his nerves, Miguel so pathetic in his new state of matrimony and with the added burden of a worthless son. Blood brother. Christ! I must be mad to even consider tying myself to such a shiftless lout, Lassiter thought angrily.

"I tell you before, Miss Ryerson," Miguel said, "they have a better selection of merchandise up at Kendall Springs than I have here."

The girl drew a deep breath, looked around, but failed to see Lassiter who was pretending to look at harness displayed behind an oversize pot bellied stove, cold now in the spring heat.

"I'm worried about Juanito, Mr. Aleman. I haven't seen him in over two weeks . . ."

"You're no good for each other. I tell you that before, Miss Ryerson. I tell your father."

"And my father agrees, no doubt," she snapped.

Lassiter watched her, his eye on a level with a stack of yard goods on a counter. So this was Charlie Ryerson's daughter. He had never met the man but knew he ran more cattle than anyone in the valley and was arrogant and bull-headed. Her dark hair was pinned up under a flat-crowned hat. She wore a flowered blouse and riding breeches of some soft material that molded them to her figure. The high polish of expensive boots was faintly dimmed by dust. A ring glittered on a finger. There was silver at her belt. Everything about her, the way she stood, shoulders back so that breasts curved at the silk blouse, the swell of hips suggested breeding and money.

"Too bad you didn't stay in California, Senorita," Miguel said through pale lips. "A little girl when you went away to school. Now a woman when you return. That is the trouble, you see. There are things you and Juanito don't understand. Your father and I lived in this valley for many years. I remember your mother. A beauty."

"Thank you for that, at least, Mr. Aleman," she said stiffly.

"Your father and I . . . we . . . what is the word . . . we *tolerate* each other. I do not want you to marry my son. It would not be good. For anyone."

"You used to like me."

"When you were a little girl, yes. I used to give you candy from the big jar when you'd come here with your mother. Do you remember?"

"I remember. I love Juanito and he loves me and I came here thinking you would help us. I haven't seen him and I'm worried . . ."

Lassiter suddenly noticed a man in the doorway leading to the dining room and saloon. One of the men who had escorted her to Aleman's Barn. How long he had been standing there, thumbs hooked in a shell belt, a faint smile on his lips, Lassiter didn't know. More of a smirk than a smile, Lassiter corrected himself. The man was about twenty-five, solidly built through the shoulders, handsome in a sly way. His features bore the dark sun stamp of men who work in the open. He wore a belted gun with bone grips. His spurs were Chihuahua, his shirt a faded red from frequent launderings.

The girl also noticed the man. "What do you want, Chick?" she demanded, wiping her eyes. Until that moment Lassiter hadn't realized the tears.

"Always figure to be close as can be, Miss Ryerson," drawled Chick. "You know, kinda like a bodyguard."

"Please tell Juanito I was here, Mr. Aleman," she flung over her shoulder to Miguel as she swept from the room. Miguel returned to the bar. Chick sauntered deeper into the store and said to Lassiter, "Who're you?"

"How long have you lived out here?"

Chick's pale eyes chilled. "Long enough. Why?"

"How come you never learned that here you don't ask a man who he is. If he wants you to know, he'll tell you."

"One of the tough ones, eh?" The smirk deepened. He had a cleft chin and a sprinkling of freckles now that Lassiter had closed distance between them to see him up close.

"Tough enough," Lassiter grunted, locking eyes.

"Any hombre who makes Miss Ryerson cry I don't like. What'd you say to her?"

"Didn't open my mouth to her, if it's any of your business."

"Me and the boys'll rope your heels together and drag you from the back of a hoss for a mile or two. That'll knock the edge off your toughness."

"Anything you want to try, let's go outside. Miguel's my friend and I don't want to see his place get shot up."

Faint uncertainty washed Chick's pale eyes. "Just don't push things, whoever you are. The Ryersons run things around here. I work for them. I look out for Miss Ryerson. Look out for her real good."

"I'm Lassiter. You can ask for me by name any time, any place. I'll be glad to accommodate."

"Lassiter?" Chick leaned forward. "Bert Monagal spoke your name recent."

Lassiter was on guard. "That so?"

"You seen him?"

Lassiter ignored the question.

"I figured him an' his boy Con would be up to Kendall Springs yesterday. But they wasn't. After roundup they always like to play some cards. Con's purty slick at it."

Here's a bastard to watch, Lassiter thought.

The Ryerson girl called to him. "Chick, I'm ready to leave."

"Be with you, Maggie . . . I mean, Miss Ryerson."

"No need for that, Chick Kelleray. To try and show this gentleman that we're closer than we are." From the doorway her dark eyes swept over Lassiter. "Or ever could be," she added. Chick Kelleray reddened.

"Soon's we sell cattle, I'll be lookin' you up, Lassiter," Chick snarled in an attempt to regain the stature Margaret Ryerson had diminished so imperiously.

Kelleray swung around on his heel and marched out of the store.

Lassiter smiled to himself, his mind clicking. Cattle sale at a ranch the size of Ryerson's meant big money. Nothing pleased him more than to try and take it away from an arrogant outfit who thought they could run everything in sight. He rubbed his hands together as if already feeling Ryerson gold between them. He walked out front where the Ryerson XR men were already in the saddle.

Margaret Ryerson and Elnora stood talking. Lassiter overheard Elnora say, "I'll tell Juanito what you said, Miss Ryerson."

Chick Kelleray heard her. Fury tightened his lips. One jealous hombre, Lassiter thought.

When they rode off, Lassiter asked Miguel about Chick Kelleray. The man had worked for XR a little over half a year and had his cap set for Margaret Ryerson, Miguel replied.

"I hope he marries her," Miguel said, staring at dust lifted by the departing XR horses.

Elnora spoke to Lassiter about Margaret Ryerson. "She was furious with Kelleray for making a fool of himself with you. She wanted you to know how she felt."

Lassiter felt that the Ryerson girl as well as the Ryerson cattle money might be an interesting project to consider. Too bad Refugio was dead. He'd have gleefully anticipated the planning and execution. Lassiter's face clouded. Execution it had been; six rifles cutting Refugio Aleman to pieces.

During the night Lassiter heard voices coming from Miguel's quarters down the hall. The Alemans were arguing again. He pulled a pillow over his head and tried to go back to sleep.

In the morning Elnora slammed a skillet on the stove when he came downstairs. Miguel was sweeping out the barroom.

"We argued again about me waiting on customers," Elnora said thinly. "I suppose you heard us."

"Just why the hell did you marry him?" Lassiter asked softly as he sprawled in a chair.

She snapped at him, repeating what she had said before. "Because I was fool enough to think I could be a partner."

"It's a look about you . . . the way you walk . . . that makes a man think it's an invitation."

"I've lived with that all my life. I have no intention of

trying to change my walk or anything else. And if a man thinks he reads an invitation, then he's a fool. And so are you for even mentioning it!"

Lassiter hadn't slept well; his mood was almost as sour as Elnora's. How he could relieve XR of cattle money had been in his thoughts most of the night. Also Margaret Ryerson's image burned across his mind; her outthrust lower lip, the saucy stride of the tall, lithe body.

"Got a feeling Miguel expected more out of you than keeping books or waiting on customers."

She met his sardonic grin. "That part of it I give gladly. Because he's been good to me. The kindest person I've ever known."

"I hope I don't hear one day that you think otherwise."

"I'll never turn on him. And it was cruel of you to suggest it."

"Realistic is all."

"What kind of grand theory now?"

"Juanito underfoot. A handsome young buck."

Anger and exasperation touched her for a moment, then she shrugged. "I've tried to be Juanito's friend. He rarely looks at me. And speaks only when he has to."

Maybe because he's in love with you, Lassiter felt like saying. Perhaps that explained why Juanito apparently had been neglecting the Ryerson girl lately.

Two days passed without Juanito's appearance. Lassiter ground his teeth. Worry lines had deepened on Miguel's dark face and an old bullet wound in his leg had flared up.

Chick Kelleray paid another visit to Aleman's Barn. This time he was alone. Kelleray was in a belligerent mood. Lassiter's mood was dark.

Lassiter saw him coming out of the bar. "Don't push anything you can't handle," Lassiter warned.

Kelleray caught him at the foot of the stairs. "Tell you this, Lassiter, anything happen to me, my brother Ed will come down here quicker'n lightning. You'll wish you was dead before he gets through with you."

"I'll remember."

"Went by to see the Monagals," Kelleray said slyly. "They got a shack in the hills an' a few head of beef."

"Cattle brands healed yet?"

"Don't know what you mean."

Lassiter's smile was cold. "Monagals were pretty good at using a running iron on another man's beef."

Kelleray pounced on Lassiter's slip of the tongue. "What'd you mean *were* pretty good? You talk like mebby they ain't around no more."

"Kelleray, you work for XR," Lassiter reminded. "A big cattle outfit. If you're even on speaking terms with cow thieves like the Monagals, it smells."

"Better talk careful, Lassiter. You ain't been so far."

"The Monagals have been run out of a dozen counties for rustling. They're accomplished cow thieves." This time Lassiter made sure not to refer to them in the past tense. But Kelleray wouldn't leave it alone.

"You bury 'em?"

"Now you're the one better talk careful."

"Ol' Bert was drunk one night up at Hopnatcher's an' he told me he aimed to salt you away first chance he got. One reason he was hangin' around up here. He said he knowed you come through here coupla times a year to see the ol' greaser . . ."

"Use that word again and you'll be gumming food for the rest of your life."

Kelleray dropped a hand to the bone grips of his

gun. Lassiter's smile was icy. "Don't try it, Kelleray." Kelleray removed his hand. But he wasn't through.

"Monagal hosses gone, when I went by their place. But damn if I didn't see 'em runnin' loose. Without saddles. I backtracked 'em. Seen where somebody stashed them saddles in the brush. An' there was marks where somebody had been diggin' in the ground recent. You kill 'em, Lassiter?"

"I came here to see Miguel Aleman, not the Monagals."

"I don't give much of a damn if you did blow their heads off. They was mean bastards."

"Were they?" Lassiter changed it. "Are they?"

"Come to think of it, when ol' Bart mentioned your name he said somethin' about a feud. Seems like I heard about it before . . ."

"Kelleray, just why the hell did you come over here this morning?"

They stood at the foot of the stairs. Some men were drinking in the bar. Elnora was cutting yard goods in the store for a rancher's wife. The Alemans had sent out word that they needed hired help. So far no response.

"I come to tell you about Maggie Ryerson," Kelleray said crossly. "I seen the way you watched her the other day. An' if you said somethin' to make her cry . . . Wa'al, I just want to tell you where I stand."

"Stand with her, you mean?" Lassiter drawled.

"In another month I'll be segundo at XR," Kelleray snapped, his temper sliding. "In six months I'll be foreman. That's when me an' Maggie get married. Now you tell that kid of Miguel's to stay clear the hell away from her. You understand that?"

"I have no intention of telling Juanito anything. He's old enough to run his own life."

"I got XR behind me, Lassiter. The biggest cow outfit in these parts. You or that goddamn greaser . . ." He changed it quickly. "That Mex give me trouble an' you'll wish you hadn't."

Lassiter had already noticed the big man glowering at Kelleray's back. The man's voice filled the room. Kelleray went dead white, as he saw the towering florid-faced man midway in the dining room, having evidently stepped from the bar. It was Charlie Ryerson, six feet tall, the once powerful frame showing signs of attrition.

"Thanks for telling me the plans you have for moving up to foreman!" Ryerson boomed. "Your plans for my daughter!"

"M . . . M . . . Mr. Ryerson. I never heard you come in."

"Go back to the ranch and draw your time."

"But, listen . . ."

"Never mind, I'll pay you off here and now!" Ryerson flung two twenty dollar gold pieces on the floor. "You haven't got a whole month coming, but I'll pay it. To be rid of you." One of the gold coins rolled under a table.

"You better not fire me, Ryerson . . ."

"I've got men with me," the rancher said in a flat voice. "I'll send your gear to Kendall Springs. You can pick it up at Hopnatcher's."

Lassiter wondered if Ryerson had overheard the part of the conversation pertaining to the Monagals. If he had, he supposed a cowman of Ryerson's stature would term their elimination on a par of ridding the range of unwanted predators.

Rage twisted Kelleray's face, draining it. "You figure I'm only a cowhand!" he shouted. "Not good enough for Maggie, huh?"

"Only two men in this world can call her Maggie. Me. And the man she marries. And it'll never be you."

Kelleray's smile was tight. "S'pose if I owned a bank I'd be good enough?"

"Buy yourself one and we'll see." Ryerson gave a sour laugh, then looked at Lassiter. "So you're Lassiter." He beckoned with a ringed finger. "Come on, I'll buy us a drink."

Lassiter didn't trust Kelleray at his back. He waited till Kelleray had stormed outside before going to join Ryerson in the bar. Ryerson and Miguel were talking together as Lassiter came up. Some XR men were in a corner of the room drinking beer from bottles.

"It isn't that I dislike Mexicans, Miguel," Ryerson was saying softly. "You know that's not true. It's just because I don't want my daughter marrying one."

"It would not be wise for Juanito to marry her," Miguel agreed quietly. "For many reasons."

Ryerson poured Lassiter a drink. "I know your rep, Lassiter. Always makes me nervous when you visit Miguel here." He smiled, but his eyes, small in the large red face, bored in coldly. There was something cruel in the eyes. The daughter's were soft brown, his hard and streaked with yellow. "I could use a tough man. You want a job?"

Lassiter let it flick across his mind. Working at XR would put him within reach of cattle sale money when the time came. But he preferred doing things his way. "Never cottoned to working for wages, Mr. Ryerson."

"Just taking the other man's money when he isn't looking, eh?" Ryerson chuckled, winked at Miguel. "I remember when he and your boy Refugio ran together. There was talk, I recollect. Two bad hombres, you. I tell you, though, I admire a fella with guts enough to take what he wants."

Lassiter matched his smile, but said nothing. *But you won't like it if I take it from you,* he was thinking.

"Just so he's not foolish enough to want mine," Ryerson finished, chuckling heartily again, as if reading Lassiter's mind. "Two things in this world I love. My daughter first, my money second. A man touch either one and . . ." Ryerson didn't finish it. He didn't need to. Lassiter knew what he meant.

"That why you fired Chick Kelleray?"

"Mainly because Margaret's taken a sudden dislike to the man. I knew he came over here this morning. I wondered why. I got an earful."

Lassiter waited for him to mention the Monagals. He didn't and the tension in his shoulders eased.

When Ryerson and his men had ridden away, Lassiter asked Miguel a question. "Why don't you think it's a good idea for Juanito to marry Margaret Ryerson?"

A pained expression touched Miguel's small dark face, framed by the gray-black hair. "Something that goes back years, Lassiter."

"Would it help to talk about it?"

Miguel pretended he hadn't heard the question.

Lassiter said, "Any gal would be happy to have a big good-looking hombre like that for a husband. Looks more Viking than Mexican. Hell, sometimes I think you must've found him in a hay mow . . ." Miguel looked so stricken that Lassiter was forced to add, "Hell, I was only joking."

That ended the discussion. Lassiter vowed he'd never bring up the subject again. Miguel was touchy when it came to Juanito's pale hair, his light gray eyes, his big frame.

One thing, while waiting for Juanito to show up, Lassiter was getting a good rest. He had plenty of food, whiskey. And a pretty woman underfoot. But unfortunately, not to touch.

That afternoon Toby Miles, a horse trader, appeared with six vaqueros and a bunch of half-wild mustangs he was trying to pass off as fully broken saddle horses. He was a short, affable man with two gold teeth. Small X scars on either cheek made Lassiter wonder if they might have resulted from the temper of a disgruntled buyer of a Miles horse.

Miles and Miguel shook hands. Lassiter was introduced and gave the man a spare nod. Lassiter was skeptical of politicians, bankers, pious females, most sheriffs and all horse traders.

Toby Miles wanted to swap horses for some of Miguel's mules. A new road was going in forty miles west and mules were in demand for the grading.

Miguel didn't have his mind on his business; his thoughts were elsewhere. He traded ten mules for six mounts of various shapes and shades that Miles hadn't been able to peddle to the cavalry.

"He's cheating you, Miguel," Lassiter pointed out later.

"It's payment, in a way," Miguel said, shaking his head. "One reason he came all this way was to bring me word about Juanito." He rubbed his small chin and stared north at the mountains.

"From the look on your face the news wasn't good."

"Toby says Juanito has been up at Kendall Springs. At Ruby's. It's a . . . a place."

Lassiter laughed. "Nothing like a good whorehouse to take the kinks out of a man. Maybe Juanito will learn to smile again."

"He's been dead drunk there."

"Whiskey goes hand in hand with a lively female."

Lassiter felt like booting the jovial little fat horse trader in the rump for ruining Miguel's day.

Juanito himself pulled in an hour later when Miles and his vaqueros were finishing the meal Elnora had cooked for them. Juanito looked like something left over from battle; he had a growth of yellow whiskers, his eyes were puffy, hollow. There was a purplish bruise on one cheek and a long cut across his forehead encrusted with dried blood. Not a deep wound, but painful. Someone had either worked him over lightly with a knife or one of the girls had used a broken whiskey bottle when he tried to get rough. Juanito was a big ungainly twenty-year-old with strength in those long arms.

Miguel gave his son a sour look. "I know where you've been. I'm ashamed of you."

Lassiter noticed that Juanito's reddened eyes were bright with anger as he looked directly at his father. But he said nothing. When he started to unsaddle, Miguel slapped the butt of the big .45 Juanito had taken to wearing lately.

"You carry a gun, you try to act tough. Toby says everybody in town was laughing about how you passed out on Ruby's porch. It took five of her girls to get you inside to a bed."

"Toby Miles said that?" Juanito glared at the corrals beyond the junk yard where Miles was barking orders to the vaqueros readying his horses and mules for the trail.

Juanito drew his gun and started toward the corral, stooping to duck under one of the poles. Lassiter caught him, pushed him back.

"Use your head," Lassiter warned. "So Toby Miles has got a loose tongue. You ever know a horse trader who didn't gossip like a woman?"

"Maybe one day I'll shoot off that loose tongue."

Some XR cowhands moving cattle to new range, had dropped in for quick beers. They were gathered at the saloon windows that overlooked the yard, listening to the exchange. One of them, a bearded man named Hal Dempster, cupped his hand and called to Toby Miles.

"Hey, Toby, you hurt Juanito's feelings." They all laughed. Miles was in the saddle, his plump legs pressed to the barrel of a big gray. He looked toward Juanito who loomed tall and angry three corrals away. Miles obviously wanted no trouble. He did not answer the XR man but moved out quickly with his herd and his vaqueros.

Lassiter was surprised to see Chick Kelleray, wearing the familiar smile, elbow Dempster out of the window. Kelleray shouted after Miles. "Tell Ruby that she better get new gals! None of us white men will take on one of them that's had that greaser in 'em for three days."

Miguel, still in the yard, turned pale. Instead of flying into a rage as Lassiter expected, Juanito gave a hollow laugh and said, "So it's even followed me here."

"What's followed you?" Lassiter demanded.

"The word you just heard, Lassiter. Be funny if I wasn't Mex after all, now wouldn't it?" Juanito flashed his father a strange look that made Miguel seem suddenly pathetic.

Juanito stormed inside and up to his room on the second floor. Lassiter went to the bar. Miguel had come in a side door with an armload of beer bottles.

"Kelleray, look around here," Lassiter said coldly. "I heard what you said about Juanito."

Kelleray winked at some of the men whose faces brightened with anticipation. "You mean you'd take on a woman that's just been had by a dirty Mex?"

"I'm gonna break your head!" Lassiter lunged. Four of the XR men grabbed him by the arms. Miguel produced his shotgun from behind the bar.

Kelleray shouted at the XR men. "Let's *all* of us jump Lassiter!"

Dempster snarled through his tangle of beard. "Fun's fun but I ain't gamblin' with no shotgun. I also ain't jumpin' Lassiter. You're the one with the big mouth. You an' him go at it alone!"

Kelleray muttered, then rode out.

"Thought he was fired," Lassiter said coldly to the XR men. "What's he doing with you?"

"He's fired, all right," Dempster grunted. "But we always kinda liked ol' Chick an' when we seen him down the road a piece we said to join us for a beer. We gotta be goin'. How much we owe you, Miguel?"

"That word greaser something you use regularly on XR?" Lassiter asked thinly.

Dempster licked bearded lips. "Reckon Chick Kelleray's the one who started callin' Juanito a greaser. Old man Ryerson just kinda picked it up when he figured Juanito was gettin' too cozy with Miss Margaret. Me, I take a man for what he is, don't give a damn whether he's Mex or what." Dempster added, "If Juanito keeps away from Miss Margaret, there won't be no more greaser talk at XR . . ."

"The girl looks old enough to make up her own mind, seems to me."

"The old man won't never see it that way. Hey, Lassiter, I got to tell you I was in Tucson the time you throwed Mike McGinty out a saloon window. Folks talked about it for a week afterwards. Hell, I couldn't even lift McGinty, let alone throw him."

The other XR men looked on Lassiter with new respect.

"Come on, boys," Dempster said, finishing his beer, "let's go move cows. The boss catch us in here he'll bust our asses."

When Miguel had gone to have a talk with Juanito, Elnora looked Lassiter over. "Quite a man, aren't you?"

"If you weren't married to Miguel," he said softly, "you'd damn soon find out I am."

"I meant throwing a man through a saloon window. I didn't mean bedroom, where I doubt if you'd excel."

Lassiter bared his teeth. "When Miguel married you he got a she-cat, claws and all."

"Perhaps," she said coolly and looked up at him out of eyes that reminded him of blue sky filled with heat lightning.

Then she hurried away, her hips swinging.

Chapter Four

Lassiter hoped Miguel had forgotten about the blood brother business. He hadn't. "Lassiter to repay me for saving your life," Miguel reminded.

Lassiter ground his teeth; Miguel hadn't saved his life at all. Bert Monagal had been leaping up from his barricade of whiskey barrels and Lassiter was spinning around after killing Con. Lassiter had the old man dead center when Miguel blew him apart with the shotgun.

Oh, hell, forget it, Lassiter, he told himself. After all, you do owe Miguel. Don't forget his dead son Refugio.

Miguel was ready for the ritual. He locked up. Elnora had retired. Lassiter almost wished she would leave with him in the morning. She wasn't doing any good here, only increasing tension between Miguel and his son. But it would hurt Miguel; he turned off the wish.

Actually, there were times when he felt a little sorry for her. But then the thought of rendezvous was always in the back of his mind, Elnora and Juanito that morning after Lassiter's arrival. Had Juanito been stricken with a guilty conscience and gone on a drunk up at Kendall Springs?

Miguel solemnly explained to Juanito what he would like to have done. "Lassiter will be your blood brother, Juanito. No, do not smile. There may come a time when you will be glad that Lassiter has taken an oath to defend your honor and . . Senor Dios forbid . . . should you come to a violent end . . . to avenge you."

"Does he mind mixing his blood with Mexican?" Juanito said with a twisted smile, looking straight into Lassiter's eyes.

Miguel got a strange look on his face. "Blood means nothing. In the eyes of Senor Dios we are all His children." Miguel and his son argued the matter in low voices. Then Juanito spoke sullenly.

"Let's get on with it," this said in English.

The ritual was performed in the old manner, a slit made with a knife in the upper arm of each man. When the blood flowed, the arms were bound together with a clean cloth and the oath recited.

". . . and I will be the same as brother to Juan Aleman, as long as we both live," Lassiter intoned.

When it was done and Juanito had gone upstairs without a word, Lassiter said, "I've done something for you, now do something for me."

Miguel was weary. "What?" he asked.

"Give Elnora a chance. Let her have the run of the place, help with the books, wait on customers. Do that in payment for me looking out for Juanito. Don't always worry because some man looks at her. She can take care of herself."

Lassiter came downstairs at what he considered an early hour, intending to build up a fire for Elnora in the stove and heat up last night's coffee for himself. He had already told Miguel he was pulling out, giving restlessness as an excuse.

"But you said you would stay a month when you first came, Lassiter," Miguel had said last night.

"I could never stay a month in one place."

"You used to when you came here."

"I'm older and things get on my nerves . . ." Lassiter tried to make a joke of it.

"You're disappointed that I married Elnora. That is it, of course." Miguel shook his head sadly.

Lassiter was surprised to find, in the faint dawn-light, that someone was downstairs ahead of him. He paused at the foot of the stairs. He had come quietly so as not to awaken anyone and they had not heard him. Juanito was slumped at the table, chin resting on his fist. Elnora leaned over him, talking earnestly in a low voice. She sensed someone's presence and jerked up to stare.

"You . . . you're up early, Lassiter," she said and he tried to decide if there was guilt in her voice or only surprise.

"I'll go outside if you and Juanito have things to say to each other."

"No need for that, Lassiter," she snapped. There was a faint sour taste in Lassiter's mouth. Well, it was none of his business; Miguel had made his bed.

Juanito gave a bark of laughter. "See, he really is my blood brother. Now he's going to run my life for me."

"Coffee's hot, Lassiter," Elnora said and poured for them all. She sat down at the table. No one spoke. Miguel came in, yawning, scratching his chest. When Elnora got up to get the coffee pot, Miguel kissed her on the cheek, having to rise to tiptoe in order to reach it.

The bitch could bend down to him, Lassiter thought angrily, instead of making him stretch up to her and look like a fool.

After finishing his breakfast, Lassiter insisted on paying Miguel for food and lodging. "I'm not exactly broke," he said with a shrug and a wink.

Miguel leaned across the table. "That business in El Paso that put you on the run. It was profitable, no?" Miguel nudged him.

Lassiter wasn't going to say anything, then saw Elnora looking at him, wiping her hands on a dishrag. Her red-gold hair had come unknotted from the steam of the stove. For some reason she looked vulnerable and he felt a need to explain about El Paso. Just why, he had no idea.

"A gambling house was set to fleece a mining engineer up from Mexico with his pockets full of Chihuahua gold. I sat in the game and beat them to it is all. The house didn't like it. They sent people after me." He smiled at Miguel, including Elnora in the smile. "I suppose your wife probably thought I robbed a rich widow."

"I thought nothing of the kind, Lassiter," she said.

Miguel twisted around in his chair to beam up at Elnora. "You two are always at each other's throats."

"He'd be at mine if he stayed around long enough," Juanito grumbled.

Lassiter shoved some gold coins across the table at Miguel, who tried to push them back. Lassiter persisted and at last Miguel sighed and started to put them in his pocket.

Elnora held out her hand. "Let me put them in the safe. And make a notation in the books. You said I could start helping you with the accounts, Miguel."

When Lassiter was ready to pull out he called Miguel outside. He reminded him about the killing of the Monagals. "Make sure your wife doesn't talk about it, old friend. And never let on to Juanito."

"My son would never talk."

"Whiskey's loosened more than one tongue," Lassiter pointed out. Miguel thought about it and then

Lassiter said, "Don't forget, you killed Bert Monagal. I'm sorry you had to get into it . . ."

"Did it to save your life . . . didn't I?"

"You did," Lassiter assured him. "Kelleray was asking questions about the Monagals. I don't like the bastard. I'll head for Kendall Springs and see if he's hanging around up there."

"Be careful of him, Lassiter."

"Next time you see Kelleray he may be wearing store teeth. Maybe it'll teach him to keep his mouth shut about names he calls certain people."

Miguel swallowed. "The Monagals are one thing, but don't fight our battles for us."

"I've got a lot of battles to fight for you, Miguel. Because of Refugio, if for no other reason. He was my good friend."

Mention of the dead son gave Miguel a moment of sadness. Then he and Lassiter gave each other the abrazo in parting. Lassiter rode north.

Elnora watched him from a window, then sank dejectedly to a chair.

Miguel started to berate Juanito for his behavior, but broke off when the younger man gave him a strange look.

"Maybe it's time to talk about my past," Juanito began, and Miguel lost color and lowered his eyes. "I've always wanted to find a link and I hunted through everything around here, but one day I found an old trunk in the attic. Hidden in the lining was a letter. It was signed Wilma and addressed to someone named Gladys. Wilma spoke of her and Chad coming west and how the baby had been born in the mountains. Wilma mentioned that the baby had yellow hair and light gray eyes. Who was this Wilma with a baby that had yellow hair and gray eyes? Seems like the letter was never mailed . . ."

"How long have you known about the letter?" Miguel asked in a dead voice.

"A long . . . a very long time."

Miguel stared out the window, hoping the departing Lassiter still remained in view. But there was no sign of him against the spring green of the hills, not even his dust.

"Why did you not mention the letter before this?" Miguel lapsed into Spanish.

"Oh, I talked about it."

Miguel blanched. "Talked about it? To who?"

"A bottle," Juanito said with a twisted grin.

Miguel straightened his shoulders, relieved that Lassiter had agreed to be Juanito's blood brother, had taken an oath. He decided it was best to try and explain the past to Juanito. With Lassiter at Juanito's side, the risks would be lessened.

Yes, it was time to speak of the years long gone.

"My son, I must tell you things that will tear my heart out by its roots. But you must listen and try not to judge too harshly . . ."

Chapter Five

Lassiter hung around Kendall Springs, keeping his ears open concerning a cattle buyer said to be due in town with a satchel full of money. Lassiter silently blessed Charlie Ryerson when he learned the cattlemen always demanded payment in cash.

This was on his mind when he saw the daughter coming along the walk. He was about to remove his hat and speak, but the high-stepping filly only gave him a cold nod and swept past him. At her side was a dour stout woman, either a friend or perhaps a housekeeper from the ranch. Lassiter went to his hotel room to put on a fresh shirt because it was time for the card games to start at Hopnatcher's and he might be there most of the night.

Margaret Ryerson was waiting for him when he stepped from the hotel. "I didn't want to talk when that woman was with me," she explained, the words gushing from the pretty mouth. "How is Juanito? I hear he got in a fight?"

Lassiter minimized Juanito's hurts, then decided to gamble on being cut cold. "If you're staying overnight in town, how about supper with me?"

"I am staying over, but supper with you would be out of the question."

Bitch, he wanted to say, then saw the stout woman emerge from the store next door and come puffing toward the girl. Margaret wheeled away, haughtily.

"He was only asking directions," Lassiter heard her say to the woman.

"You know better than to speak to a strange man on the street, Margaret. This isn't California. Your father . . ."

That was all he could hear. He was thinking how often he had used that word "bitch" lately. He would feel sorry for Elnora one minute and then the next she'd do something to turn him against her. And this Ryerson girl seemed just as bad. Concerned over Juanito one minute, then acting as if she owned the county the next.

Lassiter played a desultory game of cards. One of the players was the roly poly horse trader, Toby Miles, who smoked a cigar as odorous as the jokes he was trying to tell between hands. Lassiter sat with his back to the wall out of long habit. If any of the El Paso boys had followed him this far he wanted to see them come through the door before they saw him. He supposed it was foolish for him to stay this far south. He thought of Denver and an assayer there who owed him money. There was another consideration; her name was Bessie. He wondered if she still hung around the Gold Palace. A week with her would clear two females out of his system, Elnora Aleman and the tall Ryerson girl with the straight back and long-legged stride that put a faint bounce in her breasts that was frankly exciting.

There was to be a dance next week here at Hopnatcher's, so he learned. The place was big enough for one with the tables pushed aside. Each unmarried girl in the valley would pack a supper for two in a box. Then the box would be auctioned off and whoever bid the highest got to eat with the young lady, and dance with her, and, if lucky, escort her home. Or someplace. Lassiter was thinking of his hotel room. No, it would have to be out of town because her father could get wind of it and they might have to jump out the window and run naked into the night.

"What're you smilin' about, friend Lassiter?" Toby Miles drawled from across the table.

"Thinking of something pleasant."

"Like maybe four aces?"

"Cost you to find out, Miles." Lassiter shoved a blue chip and then a red into the pot. Other players dropped out.

The boxed suppers were supposed to be unmarked and the lucky man would have no way of knowing who the young lady was until he opened the box and found her name. Lassiter would hang around the table where the boxes were deposited and when he saw Margaret Ryerson leave hers he would surreptitiously mark it in some way so when it came up for bids he'd go the limit; the money was supposed to buy a new bell for the schoolhouse.

A faint sense of guilt nudged the door of his conscience to spoil his ruminating. She was, after all, Juanito's girl. But on the other hand, Juanito had neglected her of late. And besides, what was that old saw about there being nothing fair in love and war?

"Full house," Miles called across the table.

"Three sixes," Lassiter said and Miles raked in the pot.

"Thought you had four aces. That grin of yours lit up your whole face."

"Was thinking of a certain female. And how it'd be a real challenge to get her on her back."

"That's almost as much fun as tradin' hosses." The other two players howled with laughter and admitted that whenever Toby Miles came to town they like to split their sides every half hour or so, he was that funny.

He always arrived with a fresh supply of jokes picked up at army posts, prison camps, saloons and brothels.

"I ever tell you the one about . . ."

Lassiter saw the saloon doors pop open so vigorously that he instinctively snapped a hand to his .44. But it was the diminutive Miguel Aleman who came bounding in, not one of the El Paso crowd. Lassiter lifted a hand, started to speak, but Miguel barged right past his table, moving at a halt-trot in the barn-like place. Miguel halted, gesturing toward the bar.

"Charlie, can I see you?" Miguel called out. "Something important."

Charlie Ryerson was at the far end of the bar, his large face wreathed in tobacco smoke from the cigars he and his cronies were smoking; it curled up around the brass cones of overhead lamps, unlighted now in mid-afternoon.

Ryerson scowled, but detached himself from the bar, big watch chain jiggling at his generous curve of stomach. A half-filled glass of whiskey was gripped in a puffy hand. Smoke trailed from the cigar in a corner of his mouth.

" 'Lo, Miguel, why you in a sweat?" His speech was slurred.

"Must talk to you, Charlie. Something you've got to explain to Juanito. Can we step outside and talk?"

"Hell, this is my drinkin' day. Besides, I got nothin' to explain to that kid of yours . . ."

Miguel leaned close and spoke earnestly in a low voice. Men at the bar were staring at the pair by the windows, also those at Lassiter's table, the only one presently occupied.

Ryerson straightened up from listening to Miguel and said, "I've heard enough." He started away, but Miguel jumped in front of him. Almost like a gnat trying to block the path of an angry buffalo, crossed Lassiter's mind. But Ryerson did halt and listen to what Miguel was saying.

Ryerson said, "Nope. I'm drinkin' with the boys from Ajax Packinghouse." He gestured at two well-dressed men at the end of the bar where he'd been standing when Miguel came flying through the double doors."

"Charlie, listen to me . . ."

"They're buyin' me all the whiskey I can hold. Hopin' my telegram didn't mean what it said. But I won't change my mind. Was gonna sell 'em two thousand head of beef at thirty-seven fifty a head. But now I won't ship till fall. Don't need the money an' the grass is good. Besides, come fall the price is sure to go up."

Lassiter had been straining without success to hear what Miguel was saying to the rancher. Ryerson's words Lassiter *hadn't* wanted to hear. Through his head flashed the figures: two thousand head of beef at thirty-seven fifty a head. Seventy-five thousand dollars. A nice round sum to take galloping off to Mexico. And now Ryerson was backing out of the deal. That plus Ryerson's imperious manner with poor Miguel touched a raw nerve in Lassiter.

So far, Miguel had not spotted him in the big room. He was standing on tiptoe trying to get close to Ryerson's ear so he wouldn't have to raise his voice. He spoke desperately, loudly.

"Damn it, I want you to talk to Juanito. About that day long ago, Charlie. Back me up and explain how you and me and two other men . . ."

Ryerson's corpulent figure was suddenly stiff. "I don't know what the goddamn hell you're talking about. You been smokin' those hemp cigarettes. They do funny things to your head." Ryerson looked around, expecting laughter. Some he got, also hard grins from a few of his men at the opposite end of the bar.

Lassiter stood up abruptly, knocking over a stack of chips, the clatter loud in the suddenly stilled room. "Miguel asked to talk to you outside," Lassiter said angrily to Ryerson. "Why the hell can't you do as he asks?"

Ryerson's face flamed. Miguel spun around, his jaw dropping at sight of Lassiter's dark face. XR men tensed, awaiting word from their employer.

But before Ryerson could find his voice, Ned Hopnatcher, wearing a cracked green eyeshade, hurried from his office where he'd been working on the books. He clutched a pen that in his agitation was inking pale fingers.

"Please, boys," he pleaded, waving thin hands. "Miguel, Charlie's in one of his moods today and it's not best to cross him. Whatever you've got to say to him can wait."

Ryerson started to splutter.

Hopnatcher gave him a tight smile. "I don't want my backbar mirror shot out again. Last one cost me two hundred dollars to ship from Santa Fe . . ."

Miguel Aleman wheeled around and darted from the saloon as swiftly as he had entered.

Ryerson yelled at Lassiter. "You're a nervy bastard to talk up to me like you did . . ."

Hopnatcher clenched his wet pen in two hands in an attitude of prayer. "Please, Charlie. And you, Lassiter . . . my mirror!"

Ryerson wasn't through with Lassiter. "But I haven't made up my mind whether to have my men throw you out, or buy you a drink." He was suddenly jovial as if wishing to have everyone forget the scene with Miguel

Aleman. His bellow of laughter echoed through the big saloon. Hopnatcher looked relieved.

Lassiter went outside, jerking his hatbrim to cut the sun. He threaded his way through racked saddle horses and some wagons. Miguel had not come to town alone. Elnora was in the seat of a spring wagon, wearing a blue dress Lassiter remembered. Miguel was just untying his team.

"Was there trouble inside?" she asked anxiously. "Miguel won't tell me what happened, or even why he came to town. I . . . I just didn't want him to come alone in this state."

"Nothing happened," Lassiter assured her, then he walked over to Miguel who was holding the lines, preparing to step into the wagon. "What's this about Ryerson and Juanito?" Lassiter asked quietly so Elnora couldn't overhear.

"I'll come back in a few days when Charlie's sober. Never could talk to him when he's drunk."

Lassiter gave him a wry smile. "Don't forget I'm a blood brother to your kid."

"It is something I will never forget." Miguel tried to get into the wagon, but Lassiter held him off, leaning close.

"Damn it, Miguel, I'm your friend. What the hell did you want Ryerson to explain to Juanito?"

"Something that happened many years ago. I'll tell you one day, but not now." The dark face twisted as he glanced skyward as if to sort out answers in spring clouds. "Charlie will never admit anything. I should have known."

That was all Lassiter could get out of him except, "I must not leave Juanito alone too long these days. He . . . he is very upset."

Miguel turned the spring wagon around and headed

south toward Aleman's Barn, that lonely jumble of unpainted wood in a remote corner of the territory. Just before dust closed in on them, Elnora turned in the seat and waved to Lassiter standing in the street.

He considered going after Miguel, making him explain, but had to admit that the little Mexican could be as stubborn cold sober as Ryerson was when drunk.

Lassiter looked at Hopnatcher's sign in black letters, the front windows gleaming in the sunlight. He pondered the strange confrontation that had taken place inside, a frantic Miguel and an obstinate Ryerson over something that evidently had happened many years ago. Something that concerned Juanito.

A more prudent man might have thought twice about returning to the poker game where a handful of XR men, their mood honed by after roundup whiskey, would delight in trouble if Ryerson gave the word.

Lassiter returned to his table, sitting where he could watch not only the door, but the bar. Ryerson was busy talking to the packinghouse men.

Toby Miles leaned across the table. "Never seen Miguel so worked up in my life."

"Yeah, he was some upset," Lassiter said, passing it off.

"Something to do with his kid, I gather. I like Miguel, but his kid is no damn good. Come to a bad end, you ask me."

"I didn't ask you, Miles."

The horse trader covered it by referring to Lassiter's treatment of Ryerson. "I ever have a pet bear with a sore tooth that needs pulling, I'll get you to reach right in with a pair of pliers. Wouldn't be half as risky as you standing up to Charlie Ryerson."

The other players rewarded Miles with laughter.

Lassiter's mind was darkly on Ryerson and his pretty but stuck up daughter. No cattle money forthcoming, so he'd learned.

How far was Denver? Just over the mountains. Hello, Bessie, turn down the bed.

On a cloudy afternoon in late spring, Lassiter smiled around his cigar as he noted lust in the eye of every male jammed around the small stage at the Golden Palace, listening to Bessie Dolan. Her hair, white-gold in the spotlight, was pinned up, giving her a regal look. There might be better voices in Denver but not the sparkling personality, with a figure laced in at the waist; true hour glass.

It had been a good month for Lassiter. He'd won at faro. And he had Bessie.

Around four in the morning she let herself into his hotel room and blew her warm breath into his face, then took off her clothes. When he asked lazily what she'd been up to that night she spoke of a mine official who had let something slip about a gold shipment; too much champagne and too much Bessie had loosened his tongue.

Words of a financial nature always seemed to increase Lassiter's ardor. With the voluptuous Bessie it was doubled. After half an hour her long nails removed some of the skin from his back in her ecstasy. Finally she crumpled. Upon recovering, she opened one eye and said, "You are a bastard because you spoil me for other men."

He shrugged a bare shoulder, knowing better than to return the compliment. It always started her talking about marriage and what a great team they'd make in San Francisco.

A soft knock on the door interrupted his thoughts. Lassiter reached down from the bed and picked up his .44 from the carpet. He cocked it.

Bessie whispered suddenly in his ear. "Honey, I forgot to tell you. Three men were asking about you last night. They'd heard you patronized the Golden Palace whenever you were in Denver . . ."

Lassiter had already slid out of bed, moving soundlessly to the door when the knock was repeated. "Who is it?"

"Got a letter for you. Marked urgent." It could be the voice of the hotel clerk. It could be someone doing a pretty fair impersonation.

After all, Colorado was still in the U.S., as was El Paso, Texas. Not too far for certain people to come if their feelings against Lassiter were still smouldering.

He jerked open the door and shoved the revolver into a startled face. It was the bald room clerk, wisps of brown hair jutting over protruding ears. Lassiter looked both ways down the hall. There was no one else in sight.

Lassiter took the letter. "Thanks." He'd tip later.

The clerk stared, mouth hanging open at Lassiter in the doorway, as unclothed as the day he was born, and at the toast of the Golden Palace, sitting up in his bed, yawning.

Lassiter decided it wouldn't hurt to let him have his fill of what could be seen of Bessie. Then he closed the door slowly.

He went over to the bed and sat down. Bessie hovered over his shoulder. "When I heard the knock I remembered those men asking about you. I remember you said there'd been some trouble in El Paso, and . . . Lassiter honey, what's the *matter*?"

Lassiter was staring at Miguel Aleman's neat handwriting.

". . . Juanito has been unjustly accused of murder and is sentenced to hang on the fourteenth. I ask you to remember your oath . . ."

There was more to it; Juanito had been accused of shooting Toby Miles, the horse trader, in the back.

Lassiter got up and put on his pants. He jammed the letter into a pocket. "It happened sooner than I figured," he muttered.

Bessie brushed long blond hair away from her face. "*What* happened? What are you talking about?"

"I was a damn fool. I knew better than to be a blood brother to that wild-haired kid."

"I'll be wild-haired if you don't get back into bed with me. And don't look so grim. Smile for me and remember what I whispered to you not ten minutes ago. Our next time will be even better."

"Bessie, I'll be back in bed next time I'm in Denver."

Her eyes grew hot with anger as she watched him finish dressing. "You mean there's something more important than *me*?"

"I gave my word to somebody. I've got to keep it."

"You also gave me your word . . . about our next time . . . this very morning . . ."

"But I didn't seal it in blood."

She looked petulant for a moment, then said, "What's in that letter that's got you so steamed up?"

"Told you all I'm going to tell you, Bessie." He belted on his gun, picked up his Winchester.

She fought her anger. "Damn it, we were having so much *fun*."

"I'll be in Denver again."

She tried not to look unhappy. "What if that letter is a trap? Remember those men I told you about. They even asked Max what you looked like. So they'd be able to recognize you . . ."

"Forget it, Bessie," he said grimly, having other things on his mind.

"Honestly, those men . . ."

"They will just have to wait their turn with the other hombres who are looking for me." When he gave her a kiss and a hard grin, she tried to pull him down on her.

But he deftly broke the circle of bare arms and stepped back from the bed.

"Lassiter honey, those three men talked tough and they looked tough. Max wouldn't tell them anything, but somebody else will. You can be sure of that. Why don't we slip away to Estes Park until they leave Denver . . ."

By the time he reached the door she was screaming at him.

Chapter Six

Lassiter considered the railroad but it would land him too far east; in another year the line to the Banner County, his destination, would be finished. But it wouldn't do him any good now. He still had a week before the 14th when Juanito was scheduled to hang at Brightwater.

It was a day in late spring, clouds hanging so low over the Rockies that higher peaks were lost in frothy white. He was alternately damning himself as he rode south, for becoming involved with Miguel Aleman's offspring, and a deep sympathy for Miguel himself.

He was so preoccupied with the tragedy that would face him when he reached the jail where Juanito was imprisoned, that his sharp gaze was not as intent on the trail ahead as usual.

It was late afternoon and he'd been pushing hard.

A big man on a bay horse, wearing a tipped back sweated hat, a faded blue vest and worn dungarees, suddenly rode out of a brushy draw.

"Howdy," he called. "Denver nawth of here or south?"

The man had a flat nose and small eyes. Lassiter had never seen him before. He was armed with a holstered brown-butted revolver and a booted carbine.

"North." Lassiter had reined in twenty feet from the man. He jerked a thumb over his shoulder. "I just came from there."

He slowly closed the gap between them, noting insincerity in the smile the stranger flashed. Short hairs on the back of Lassiter's neck began to twitch when he heard a faint click of a shod hoof on rock somewhere behind him on the trail. He wasn't fool enough to look around.

Lassiter rode up to the big man on the bay horse, who was still smiling. Then he rode around him so that the man had to turn his horse.

"Don't get so suspicious, Lassiter," the man said, his grin now showing strain. "Hell, I only wanted a word." The two horses stood head to head but it was the stranger who presented shoulder blades for a target for somebody on the backtrail instead of Lassiter.

Lassiter said, "What name did you call me?"

The man's small eyes blinked and he seemed perplexed and more nervous than before. "You are Lassiter, ain't you?"

"My name's Bastanchury. Sheepman with a spread over by Hammer Mountain."

"Fella at the Golden Palace described you . . ." The man broke off as Lassiter drew his .44.

"Thought you didn't know where Denver was," Lassiter said coldly.

"Then you are Lassiter."

"You say it real loud so your friend or friends can hear. How many downtrail? One, two, half a dozen?"

The man stared, licked his lips.

"Your two friends figured to get a gun at my back while you and me palavered. Well, it didn't work out that way. It's your back to the guns now, not mine."

"You're loco to think that, Lassiter." The man was obviously tough enough, but lacking experience. "I got no friends along with me."

"Bessie said there were three of you. I didn't pay any

attention. Seems I should have." Here the trail was narrow, between steep brushy hills. "Tell your friends to show themselves. Or I'll blow you right out of that saddle."

"I tell you, I'm alone . . ."

In desperation the man tried to spur his bay horse, but Lassiter was ready. He caught the animal by a headstall, dragging it down. His own mount was skittish but under control. Lassiter rammed his gun barrel into the stranger's gut at the lower wings of the unbuttoned blue vest. The man's face lost color.

"We was paid to only cripple you up, Lassiter," the man said in an attempt at bravado, "but now you're makin' it bad for yourself."

"You got it wrong, friend. You're the one in trouble." Lassiter jabbed him again with the .44. "Who the hell are you?"

"Quincy . . ." His breath faded as Lassiter punched him in the gut again with the weapon. He cried out. Lassiter disarmed him, throwing the weapons overhand into the brush above the trail.

"Tell your friends to show themselves," Lassiter repeated. *"Now!"* Or you're dead, Quincy."

Quincy had barely enough breath left, but he managed. "Freddie, Sam!" turning his head slightly so that his voice carried back up the trail, past towering slabs of rock greened in spots with lichen.

Lassiter heard faint sounds of voices; two men arguing.

"Tell 'em, Quincy!" Lassiter ordered again.

"You heard him! He's got me covered, damn it. He means business!"

Two riders reluctantly pushed their horses into view uptrail. One of them was brown-bearded, lodgepole thin, his companion red-faced and with the kind of belly that reminded one of a gunny-sack filled with sand. Both men looked sullen, angered. They held rifles but had the good sense to sit with the barrels slanted at the ground and not at Lassiter.

"Drop the rifles, boys, or you'll have to find a shovel to bury Quincy."

The one with the brown beard yelled at Quincy. "Why in hell'd you let him get a drop on you!"

"I made a mistake, Freddie," Quincy shouted back, eyes flicking between Lassiter's hard face and the gun muzzle only twelve inches from his blue vest. "You an' Sam have made a few mistakes yourselves . . ."

Lassiter rapped out his command again: *"Drop those rifles!"*

The pair let their weapons fall, careful to pick a spot where the dust was thick so they would not be damaged on a rock. Obviously they meant to retrieve the rifles later; Lassiter had other plans for them. He ordered Freddie and Sam to ride toward him. When they were ten yards away from the rifles they had dropped, he told them to halt.

"You, Freddie, unbuckle your gunbelt. Let it fall."

Freddie hesitated; Quincy screamed at him. "Do it, for Christ's sake!"

And when the holstered revolver and shell belt had plopped into the trail dust, Lassiter ordered Sam to follow suit.

"Look, Lassiter," Sam began to whine, "we don't mean you no harm . . ."

"Cripple me, your friend Quincy said. Drop that gun, damn you. Once it's in the dust then I want to know who the hell hired you."

Sam had the rangy build that denoted speed. He used it, whipping up the revolver he had been ordered to discard. At the same moment Freddie plunged off his horse headfirst, rolling, his intention to grab the gun he had been forced to drop and start firing. Quincy tried desperately to rip Lassiter's revolver out of his hand. Lassiter slammed him across the face with it, ripping open a cheekbone. As he fought for balance, arms windmilling, he was in the direct line of Sam's first shot. Lassiter whipped around in the saddle as he heard the lethal slap of a bullet smashing into human flesh. Quincy's eyes were already dimming as Lassiter spurred aside and squeezed trigger an instant before Sam fired again. Sam's bullet screamed harmleslsy off a boulder midway up the hillside. He was already off balance, Lassiter's bullet having caught him in a shoulder. Impact twisted him in the saddle. Hurt as he was, Sam awkwardly tried to bring up his gun for another try. He was grimacing with the lips of a mouth filled with horse teeth. There was a sudden gap in the teeth from Lassiter's second shot. Sam toppled, his horse rearing.

Without losing a beat, Lassiter rode directly at Freddie who was on all fours and just coming up with the gun Lassiter had forced him to drop. But before he could get set, Lassiter's mount bore down on him. Desperately Freddie tried to roll out of the way. A foreleg caught him in the ribcage, knocking him into a clump of sage. A scream broke from the man's lips. Then it became a whimper.

Lassiter reined in and looked around. Sam lay with one arm outflung, his open mouth staining the dust a dull brown. Some distance down the trail Quincy was motionless, a leg twisted under the heavy body. Lassiter had seen enough death to recognize it here on this lonely trail through rough country. He reloaded, then swung down to bend over the survivor. He kicked the man's gun out of reach. "Who hired you, Freddie?"

"Your damn hoss . . . busted ribs, sure as hell . . ."

"The three of you together didn't have brains enough to fill the watch pocket of a midget," Lassiter said in disgust.

"Shoulda killed you right off . . . way to do it . . . I told him that when he hired us, but he didn't want the law . . ."

"Let me hear a name. Who the hell hired you?"

"You . . . you'll find out. Them's our kinfolk you killed . . ."

Lassiter had had enough. He leveled his gun at Freddie's head. "I asked a name. I want it."

Freddie's breathing had eased, but his lips were still white with pain. He stared at the gun pointed at his left eye and said, "Ed. Ed Covey."

"Why'd he want me crippled up? To keep me from doing what?" Lassiter cocked his .44. "Two of your foolish friends are dead. Speak up."

"Kinfolk, I told you . . ."

"I just as soon make it a clean sweep, Freddie."

Freddie struggled to an elbow, pain washing the last color from his face. "Covey wanted you beat up bad. But we had to be sure you was the right man. We got the wrong man on a job we done for Ed once. We didn't want to make another mistake . . ."

"Why'd this Ed Covey pay you to jump me?"

"Never said," Freddie gasped. "Only that he didn't want you to leave Colorado for a spell."

At first Lassiter had thought it was some jealous swain who had resented his attention to Bessie. "This have something to do with Miguel Aleman's kid being in trouble?"

"All I know is what I told you, Lassiter." Freddie seemed suddenly weary, his voice so low Lassiter could barely hear him. "There's a canteen on my horse. Will you get me a drink? I'm all tore up inside."

"All of a sudden you're too sweet for words." Lassiter's lips twisted. He leaned down, patted along the man's belt and felt a metallic bulge under the overhang of belly. He ripped open the shirt and pulled out a derringer.

"Right between the shoulder blades when I turned around to get you that drink of water. You're no smarter than your dead friends."

Freddie Peal sagged back on an elbow, grinding his teeth in anger and frustration. "You started something today, Lassiter. If it takes twenty years, me an' Ed an' the rest of our kinfolk will run you to the ground."

"I'm an old hand at feuds, Freddie. You don't scare me much. Ed Covey, you said his name was, eh?"

"You'll meet up with him. Meet up with his kid brother, too. Them two is closer'n laces in a miner's boot, Ed is always sayin'. An' that little brother is ridin' high now an' Ed figures you might bust up the kid's game, whatever it is."

"What's the name of this brother?"

But Freddie had passed out from the savage pain that had been inflicted by a foreleg of Lassiter's plunging horse. Had the horse struck other than a glancing blow it would have caved in the rib cage.

Lassiter looked at him crumpled in the dust, left side of his shirt ripped from the shod hoof, the flesh scraped raw and bleeding. Not much of a threat now. He lowered the hammer on his gun.

"Was a time, amigo, when maybe I'd have put a bullet in your head just for luck," Lassiter muttered. "Maybe I've mellowed some." He gave the unconscious

Freddie a nasty grin. "You'll have to get your own drink of water. And bury your two friends."

Buzzards, with the uncanny telegraphy they had worked out with the Angel of Death, were already beginning to circle overhead. If Freddie didn't regain consciousness soon, there would be precious little left of his two friends to bury.

Lassiter gathered up their weapons, unloaded each one, then rode on. He was taking no chance. He'd survived one blood feud. He didn't like it that today might see the start of another. He dumped the empty weapons in a ravine and rode on. He'd already wasted enough time today. There weren't hours to spare; all too soon Juanito Aleman was to go to the gallows.

Lassiter arrived at his destination on Friday the thirteenth. It seemed like a bad omen. Juanito was to hang Saturday morning. Twenty-four hours or less.

The courthouse of Brightwater, seat of Banner County, was adobe as were half the other buildings along Center Street. The others, including the two-story hotel, were frame.

Lassiter stabled his horse and entered the hotel. He asked for a room. A clerk wearing a white shirt with a dirty collar, rented him the last one.

"Plenty of folks here for the hangin'," the clerk volunteered, accepting Lassiter's two dollars. "You here for the show?"

"I hear it's a Mex kid murdered somebody."

"Shot Toby Miles in the back. Miles was a hoss trader."

"Think I met him once."

"You ever had dealings with Toby, you'd sure remember him." The clerk chuckled, then sobered. "He was a mighty sharp trader, but wasn't no reason for Aleman's kid to gun him down."

"Must have had a reason, though."

"Plain cussedness. The Aleman kid's got a scary temper. Most Mexicans around here are small. This one seems big as a barn door, damn near as wide. He don't look Mex, but he's sure got the blood of the meaner ones I've run into out here."

"I've run into a few mean whites, a few mean Indians."

The clerk was staring at Lassiter's signature. "I remember you from New Orleans. The time you an' Duke Henry tore up that riverboat." He put a thin hand across the desk for Lassiter to shake.

Maybe you won't be so happy to remember I gave you my hand to shake, Lassiter thought grimly, if I have to bust Juanito out of that jail.

He needn't have worried too much about it for within the hour he was fairly well convinced that Juanito Aleman was guilty as charged and should pay the penalty. Still . . . He pressed on, asking his questions. Some of them concerned the Ed Covey who had hired three men to waylay him south of Denver. But no one in saloons or stores that Lassiter questioned had ever heard of Ed Covey. Nor did they know of any brother named Covey who might reside in Banner County.

There didn't seem to be much to that lead, Lassiter had to admit.

He kept an eye open for Miguel Aleman, wondering if his friend would come to town for the execution of his son. For sure, Miguel wasn't registered at the hotel. After it was over, Lassiter vowed, he'd get drunk with Miguel and try to get him over the loss of his son.

Miguel's young wife, Elnora, crossed his mind; he wondered how she was taking this tragic turn of events. What would the loss mean to her? Losing a stepson? Or perhaps a lover, remembering his earlier suspicions.

Sheriff Tod Lambert was out of town for the afternoon, so Lassiter learned when he tried to see the prisoner.

The deputy in charge, a nervous chunky man named Morton, refused to give Lassiter permission. "Sheriff Lambert won't let nobody in."

"I'd like a word with the sheriff."

"He ain't here. Went to visit his sister. Hell of a time for a woman to get sick. Tod's sure got his hands full."

"How's the prisoner bearing up?" Lassiter asked.

"Surly bastard, can't get nothin' outa him."

"You think he's guilty?"

"Ask me, he shoulda hung long ago."

"He's killed before this?" Lassiter asked in surprise.

"Naw, but he's such an ornery bastard. When a Mex goes bad, there ain't nobody worse. Sheriff oughta be back around sundown. But don't think he'll let you in to see the prisoner. We got a long night ahead of us. Hangin' is at dawn."

Lassiter had already learned that there was no chance to speak to Juanito through his cell window. A high board fence shut off any view of the death cell. At least Juanito wouldn't be pestered by the curious as Lassiter had seen happen before.

He prowled the crowded town looking for a cafe where he could get an early supper. He needed a full stomach to brace himself for the ordeal ahead. An obligation to see Juanito for the last time. He owed it to the dead brother, Refugio. He owed it to the father, Miguel.

He found a Chinese cook deftly turning a big steak over a fire of mesquite logs in a cafe window. A double size with fried potatoes was what he needed. His stomach had rumbled most of the way south from Denver.

It had been a bad month for Charlie Ryerson. His own daughter refused to speak to him because he would not allow her to visit the county seat and spend the night with her friend Jennifer. She stormed and raged, then burst into tears the day he confined her to the ranch. The formidable housekeeper, Mrs. Hopkins, had been ordered to see that Margaret stayed in her wing of the big ranch house. He knew very well it wasn't Jennifer she wanted to visit, but Juanito in his death cell.

How many times had he told her Juanito Aleman was not for her. And now he had been proved right. Juanito had murdered a man and the evidence was conclusive. Even she couldn't deny that.

He didn't want his daughter up at Brightwater sobbing over a condemned murderer. There was too much at stake. Charles Baxter Ryerson's name had been mentioned as a possible replacement for the territorial governor, a man suffering from a long illness.

It was not a time for scandal. Especially scandal from the past. Only a few more days and Juanito Aleman would hang and it would be over. Thank God!

He went outside to give orders to his new foreman, Hal Dempster. In the back of his mind he was wondering how long Dempster would last on the job. Others hadn't. Next time he hired a foreman he'd get an ex-Cavalry sergeant who would whip the crew into line.

He saw a familiar figure riding up the tree-lined ranch road. Miguel Aleman looked like a midget in the saddle of a big-boned gray.

"Charlie, I have to speak to you."

Ryerson jerked his head, walking toward some cottonwoods, away from any of his men who might eavesdrop.

"I know you've come about your son," Ryerson said, composing his features into the familiar mask that was supposed to intimidate. Miguel didn't seem cowed.

"You are my only hope, Charlie. You know all the important people at the capital . . ."

"I can't help your son. A jury found him guilty and a judge sentenced him to hang."

"But he is not guilty."

"What proof do you have, Aleman?" Best to use the last name, keep the bandy-legged little fool in his place.

"A feeling—I have here." Miguel placed a hand over his heart. Ryerson almost pitied the man and his pathetic gesture of faith in the face of monumental evidence.

"Even the kid's own lawyer thinks he's guilty."

Miguel Aleman drew a deep breath, tilted up on his toes to give him more height. It didn't help; it never had.

"I beg for your help, Charlie."

"I don't want to argue about it, Aleman. I've told you, I can do nothing."

"I learned that you bought dinners and whiskey and cigars for the jurors. The judge is your friend, Charlie. You put the sheriff in office . . ."

"Don't try and say I influenced a verdict. Your son is guilty. Everybody knows it . . . but you." Ryerson shook his head. "Somewhere in your family there's a strain of mad dog that Juanito inherited."

Miguel's eyes brightened with anger, desperation. "You *know* that is not so!"

"I know nothing . . ."

"Don't you remember that day? A long time ago, but you can't have forgotten that day. You lost some blooded stallions and somebody said those drifters had them . . ."

"That's enough!"

"We all wanted to help you find those horses, Charlie. And we did find your best horse with those drifters . . ."

"Shut up!" Ryerson's roar carried to his men who were some distance away, receiving orders from the foreman. They looked across the yard in surprise at the pair in the cottonwoods.

"We shot those drifters when they resisted, Charlie," Miguel persisted in Spanish, clinging with both hands to a thick arm when the cattleman tried to stalk away in the indignation he hoped covered his fear.

Ryerson spun around. "You're losing your mind!" he shouted. "It's strain over your son . . . enough to unsettle anyone, I admit, but don't try and involve me . . ."

"Charlie, you are involved!"

Miguel made a clumsy attempt to draw a weapon. Ryerson pinned his arms. "Go home, Aleman," he said in a low, trembling voice. "You keep your mouth shut. Or I'll burn down Aleman's Barn, so help me. Your widow won't even have a roof over her head. She'll be alone, defenseless. A young woman like her, pretty and vulnerable. A widow."

"Help me, Charlie, damn you, *help* me!"

"If you have even a shred of love for that woman, keep your mouth shut. *Shut!* I'll break her, Aleman, to the point where she'll beg somebody to kill her. Or she'll take her own life."

Again the small brown hand moved, but this time Ryerson jerked free the weapon from beneath the old

Mexican's coat. He flung it into the trees. Then he struck Miguel on the point of the jaw. Miguel collapsed without a sound.

"Send him home in a wagon," he ordered his foreman. "If he keeps on raving like this we'll have to see that he's put away someplace where they can keep him in chains. The crazy stories he's trying to tell. When he comes to he may be violent. He may have to be restrained."

Hal Dempster, latest in a long line of XR foremen, fired for one reason or another for displeasing their employer, jerked his bearded chin in assent. "He get violent, we'll handle him."

"See that you do."

As Ryerson stalked away, Dempster considered the fine line between a beating and outright murder. Although he wanted to please the boss, he didn't want to end up on a gallows as Juanito Aleman was about to do.

Chapter Seven

By the time Lassiter finished his meal, the sheriff had returned from a visit to his ailing sister. Perquisites of office, free food and liquor, were reflected in the flab that padded Sheriff Tod Lambert's six foot frame. Lassiter judged him to be around fifty. Lambert was under the gallows with the hangman. They were inspecting the trap door. Some of those in the crowd of interested spectators offered advice, which both men ignored.

"Hinges bind," the hangman grunted, his voice as sour as the expression on his long face. In bowler hat and dusty black suit he might be taken for a frontier undertaker. His profession was certainly a contributor to that trade. A coffin, discreetly covered with an Indian rug, was in one corner beneath the shadowed gallows platform.

Lassiter saw that Brightwater was filling up with rigs of every description. Families were evidently going to make a picnic out of it. They were camped under big trees in a clearing, building cookfires. Sparks in the twilight danced into heavy branches overhead. Obviously these people did not mind their children witnessing the macabre drama scheduled for dawn, fathers no doubt believing that to watch a man die at the end of a rope would be a deterrent to young sons who might in the future consider wandering from the path of law and order. As for the young daughters, mothers would no doubt make sure that in the tragic moment they were forbidden to look. Many would, of course, their memories seared for a lifetime by what they had witnessed under the rising sun in the county seat of Banner County.

Lassiter found a chance to introduce himself to the sheriff. Lambert looked him over carefully out of steel gray eyes. The sheriff grumbled about the carpentry these days. "Give Homer twenty dollars to build this here scaffold an' damn if he didn't hang the trap door so that the hinges bind. Sure can't have that."

"Spoil all the fun for the audience."

"Mebby wouldn't exactly spoil their fun," Sheriff Lambert chuckled, missing the irony, "'cause he'll hang if it takes us an hour to get the damn trap workin' right. What'd you say your name was?"

Lassiter repeated it, although he sensed Lambert had caught his name the first time.

"Seems like I heard of you," the sheriff said.

"Probably."

"Old man Aleman claimed you'd likely be showin' up sooner or later. Blood brother, Miguel called you."

"He in town?"

"Naw, he's laid up down at Aleman's Barn."

"What happened?" Lassiter demanded thinly.

"Wife claims somebody beat him up. But the XR boys claimed they found him layin' in the road. Likely his hoss throwed him. Must've got spooked by a rattlesnake or somethin'."

"Maybe."

The sheriff's lips curled. "Damn bad choice you made, bein' blood brother to the likes of Juanito Aleman."

"What if he's not guilty?" Lassiter said and as Sheriff Lambert started to bristle, "Juries have been known to make mistakes."

"Not this time, by god." Gray eyes were bright with

anger. As Lassiter met his glare, the eyes lost their belligerence. Lambert said in a quieter voice, "Most times a man talks up like you done, I'd . . ." His smile was weak as he broke off, massaging his large right fist. "But you bein' Juanito's blood brother, reckon you want to believe him innocent. Just like his pa swears Juanito wouldn't kill a man. Fact is, he did."

The sheriff sketched the crime for Lassiter while the hangman, a few feet away, worked impatiently with the trap door. He had the assistance of two men who would get under the trap, push it into place. Then the hangman would climb the thirteen steps and pull the release lever. Sometimes the trap crashed, jarring the grisly structure, at other times it was stuck.

"His weight'll likely push it down," the hangman called to Sheriff Lambert. "How much you say he weighs?"

"Right around one seventy."

"Feed him a good last meal an' it'll be enough," the hangman said icily. Some of the onlookers roared with laughter.

"You were saying?" Lassiter prompted Sheriff Lambert.

"Let's get away from that damn noise. I claim the town oughta build a good gallows an' let it stand. But no, most folks want it tore down each time. Claim it looks bad for the town. Wa'al, to get back to your blood brother . . ." The sheriff halted by a store front, leaned back, beefy shoulders against 'dobe, thumbs hooked in his belt. His badge of office shone dully in the last of the sunlight, red-gold through the trees. A clerk wearing sleeve holders climbed on a stool to put a flaring match to a kerosene entrance lamp over the doorway.

"Juanito an' this hoss trader, Toby Miles, had trouble early this year," the sheriff was saying. "Got in a fist fight. Wa'al this time when Toby come through, it seems Juanito wanted to pick up where they left off. Only this time the Mex kid had a gun. Him an' Toby went outside Hopnatcher's. Miles knocked him down, was walkin' away. There was a gunshot. Miles fell dead. Shot in the back."

"Who saw it?"

"There's been bad blood between Juanito an' Toby Miles for months, like I said . . ."

"Must have been some witnesses," Lassiter tried again.

"You ask me, the kid started to go bad when Miguel took hisself a new wife. My ol' lady claims it's downt right immoral for a man his age takin' on a young filly, an' a looker at that. Juanito started drinkin' too much . . . I mean more'n he ever did. He ain't never exactly been a stranger to a bottle since he's been old enough to ask his way to the nearest saloon." The sheriff smiled, awaiting Lassiter's response to cow country humor. Lassiter's face was a mask.

"Witnesses, Sheriff. Who the hell saw Juanito kill that horse trader?"

"Now I been givin' you leeway on account of you bein' a blood brother. But don't you go raisin' your voice to me."

"I only asked a question."

"I can have ten men swarmin' over you afore you can say spit . . ." The sheriff's voice faded away under Lassiter's hard gaze. He wiped a drop of saliva from the lower lip, evidence of the tirade he had decided to terminate. "Mick Maxwell, swamper at Hopnatcher's for one; he was a witness. Went out to empty a bucket an' swears he seen Juanito pull a gun an' shoot Miles right through the X where his suspenders crossed."

"Anybody else?"

"Chick Kelleray. Used to work for XR Cattle Company."

"Only two witnesses?" Lassiter asked quietly, remembering Chick Kelleray with the smirk, who had talked about Margaret Ryerson within earshot of her father. And been fired for it.

"When everybody run outside after the gunshot, Juanito was holdin' the gun that killed Toby Miles. One shell fired. Slug dug outa Miles was a forty-five. Same as them left in Juanito's gun."

Which only confirmed what Lassiter had heard from others in town he had questioned about the murder. They all thought. Juanito deserved to hang.

"I'd like to see the prisoner. Give me ten minutes or so," Lassiter requested. "That'll take care of the blood brother business."

"Kinda wish you'd never gone into it?" The sheriff gave him a wise look. Lassiter shrugged and the sheriff said, "You can have fifteen minutes, Lassiter. How's that?"

Lassiter said he appreciated the generosity. He tried to think of something he could bring Juanito. What would he really like. All Lassiter could think of, in Juanito's case, was whiskey.

"Can I take him a bottle?" Lassiter asked.

Sheriff Lambert massaged his chin with thumb and forefinger, thinking it over. "Let him get drunk, you mean?"

"Won't be the first time a sheriff has let his prisoner have the last hours with a bottle."

"Small bottle, only a pint. Not a quart. He can't handle whiskey no better'n an injun can."

"An Indian can't handle it because he tries to drink up every drop before somebody takes it away from him," but it was lost on the sheriff.

"Juanito has likely got injun blood, all Mexes has got injun blood." Passersby turned to look at them together in front of the store. The sheriff said, "I admit Juanito sure don't look Mex, though. But two or three drinks an' he goes kinda loco."

Lassiter thanked the sheriff, then went to the nearest saloon to make his purchase. There the crowd talked of nothing but the hanging tomorrow. Some of the men grumbled that they'd come a long distance for the festivities and planned to stay up late drinking. They didn't see why the sheriff couldn't have the hanging at noon as well as at dawn.

"Give us a chance to get more shut eye," as one man put it, pulling at his suspenders. There was laughter. Everyone in a jovial mood for Juan Aleman's exit from mortality.

As Lassiter made his way toward the jail he overheard some women discussing the crime. "I feel for the young man," one of them said confidentially to the others, "but there ain't a doubt in the world but that he kilt that poor Mr. Miles."

"I feel sorry for Miguel Aleman," another woman said. "He's the one sired that young demon."

"Not since he took that good-lookin' young wife, I don't feel sorry for him," snipped a plump woman in a wrinkled brown dress. " 'Tis a sin for a man to marry a woman only a shade older than his own son."

"My Harry says this'll be the first time they ever hung a pale-haired Mexican in the territory."

Some of the women tittered.

A sardonic smile touched Lassiter's lips as he went on down the street. There weren't many people about, it being the supper hour. For those people a hanging was a fiesta, a time to renew acquaintances, gossip with neighbors seen only a few times a year, then hitch up and head for home.

Lassiter announced himself at the jail door. It was still daylight but already two flaring kerosene lamps bathed the front of the jail with yellow light.

"Let him in, Clyde," Sheriff Talbert called jovially.

Clyde Morton, the stocky deputy Lassiter had seen earlier, tucked a sawed-off shotgun under his arm and unbarred the jail door. He was the only one on duty besides the sheriff. The other two deputies had gone home to eat. It would be a long night.

Several men were seated at an oak table in the jail office, drinking and smoking cigars. Sitting apart from the others was the hangman, who looked Lassiter over with a professional eye.

Probably as a possible future client, guessing weight, Lassiter thought grimly.

He was a little surprised to see Charlie Ryerson overflowing a chair, a cigar clamped between his teeth. Ryerson gave Lassiter a curt nod. "Didn't expect to see you here, Lassiter."

"I'm lettin' him take a bottle to our prisoner," the sheriff said.

Ryerson knocked ash from his cigar onto the stone floor. "Aleman doesn't deserve the luxury of whiskey."

"Charlie, Charlie," soothed Sheriff Talbert. "Won't do no harm. Just figure how lucky you are." The sheriff grinned slyly. "'Cause after tomorrow you won't have to worry none about your daughter marryin' that son-of-a-bitch. Beggin' your pardon, Lassiter, I plumb forgot you're his blood brother." They all laughed except Ryerson and the hangman.

Lassiter checked his temper.

Sheriff Lambert took the bottle from Lassiter, removed its wrapping of newspaper. "Just wanta make sure you ain't smugglin' in no hacksaw blade."

It crossed Lassiter's mind that this sheriff was the type of oaf who donned blackface and appeared in minstrel shows. For sure, Lambert had an appreciative audience in six of the men, including the stocky deputy, Clyde Morton. Only Ryerson and the hangman were unsmiling; the latter probably anticipating the fifty dollars the county would pay him for dropping Juanito Aleman into eternal darkness, as the Bible shouters put it, at sunup Saturday morning.

"Remember seeing you at Aleman's Barn," Ryerson said, scowling up at Lassiter who now had the unwrapped bottle back in his possession. "Happened to remember later how tough you are."

"How you know he's tough, Charlie?" drawled a freckled man with a red mustache.

"He tangled with a friend of mine some years back. Mel Saunders. Remember, Lassiter?"

"Yeah. I moved some cattle across his range once. He didn't like it."

"Maybe because you not only moved some of yours, but also some of his." Ryerson winked at the others. Lassiter decided to let pass the reference to the possibility he might be a cow thief. In reality he had been, at times. Probably would be again. Ryerson hadn't accommodated him by selling cattle so as to make available a satchel of cash money. But Ryerson had cows. The border wasn't too far. Lassiter had Mexican friends who didn't worry too much about brands on Anglo cattle. Ryerson was trying to bait him; Lassiter only smiled.

"Go get your visit over with, Lassiter," the sheriff said. "You got fifteen minutes. Clyde, you go unlock the door for him. An' you stand down the hall just in case. You hear?"

"Yeah, Tod, I hear." Clyde Morton slung his sawed-off shotgun under one arm and removed a large brass key from his pocket. He jerked his head at Lassiter.

Charlie Ryerson shifted his bulk, putting a creaking strain on the chair legs. "Tod, you going to let Lassiter go in that cell with a *gun*?"

Tod Talbert had been about to raise a glass of whiskey to his lips. He set it down, blinked at Ryerson. "Wa'al, I never thought much about it. With all of us settin' right here he couldn't do much."

"My friend Saunders once said that if you give Lassiter an inch, he'll take not only a mile but half the county along with it."

"Hey, Charlie, that's purty good," one of the men chuckled. "Half the county, by god." He slapped his knee.

"Tod, you've got wet sawdust in your head instead of brains," Ryerson growled, "if you let him go in there armed."

The sheriff reddened at the insult but tried to cover his embarrassment. "Plumb slipped my mind, to tell the truth, Charlie. Thanks for pointin' it out. Guess I'm wore out. The trial an' all and my sister bein' sick an' my Ella over there nursin' her. Lassiter?" The sheriff held out his hand for the gun.

Lassiter was smart enough to make no protest; it would solve nothing. Besides, he had expected to be disarmed. And he had just about made up his mind; he wasn't here to help a prisoner escape. He was here only because he had sworn an oath, done against his better judgment, but done nevertheless.

As he followed the deputy down the narrow hallway he was wondering how many others in Banner

County could insult the sheriff as Charlie Ryerson had just done and not pay for it later. As in other counties, he supposed it depended on a man's bank account, the extent of his political power. From what Lassiter had heard, Ryerson apparently had both.

From the jail office the corridor was straight for fifteen feet, then bisected a longer hallway. To the left a drunk was singing off key in one of the ten cells in that wing. To the right at the end of the hall was the single cell holding Juanito. Lassiter heard the voices of the men in the office become a murmur. Deputy Morton marched like a Prussian, boots thumping on stone. Lassiter glanced over his shoulder. Down the dim hall the cells of the other wing were closed off by a solid door. Nor could he see the office, only the faint wash of lamplight competing with fast fading daylight.

Clyde Morton unlocked the cell door with a great clanking of the key. The barred door squealed open, banged shut at Lassiter's back. He was locked in. Clyde tramped off down the hall several paces and halted. He leaned against the wall, waiting.

Juanito stood at the barred window, his back turned, looking out at the faint afterglow in the sky, visible above a high board fence, the last twilight he was scheduled to see. His uncut yellow hair was rumpled, the back of his white Sunday shirt sweat marked. A tray of uneaten food rested on a small table. There was no knife, fork or spoon. Evidently Sheriff Lambert was taking no chances on his prisoner using one of them for a weapon. A man ready to hang could eat with his fingers like an animal. Along one wall was a cot and under it a night jar.

"Juanito, I brought you a present."

"Sheriff told me you'd be along with it. Thanks for nothing, Lassiter."

An oath crowded out of Lassiter's throat which he checked at the lips; this was no time to curse a man who was about to die.

He pressed the bottle on him. "It'll ease the time till you . . . have to go."

Juanito stared at the bottle in his two hands as if it might have been some curious artifact from a forgotten civilization. Without warning he hurled it against a wall. Shattered glass was loud in the stillness. Whiskey spread down the wall and across the floor. The air reeked of good whiskey. Clyde Morton with his shotgun came pounding along the hallway, followed in a moment by Sheriff Lambert and some of his cronies from the office.

"What the hell was that!" the sheriff bellowed through the bars. He stared at the shards of glass, the stain of whiskey on the floor.

Lassiter did not turn his head. He told Sheriff Lambert that Juanito had not wanted whiskey and in rage had smashed the bottle.

"Still got that goddamn Mex temper, ain't he?" one of the men observed. Odor of alcohol stung the nostrils.

"Not for long he ain't got that temper," the sheriff corrected. "Lassiter, you better step outa there. Seems like he ain't in no mood for company."

"You promised me fifteen minutes with him."

The sheriff pulled at a watch, squinted in the faint light. "You already wasted time. All right, Clyde, leave him be." They walked away.

"I thought you'd be glad to get your hands on some whiskey," Lassiter said when they were alone again.

"I hate the damned stuff. But something drives me to it."

"Because your father took on a new wife?"

"My *father*?" Juanito spat with unexpected vehemence, followed by strangled laughter.

"He's been good to you, for Christ's sake . . ."

"Can't deny that and I never have."

"Sometimes you sound like you hate him."

"He's not my father."

"That's a damn fool thing to say. What gave you that idea?"

"He told me."

Lassiter had been kicking aside some of the broken glass. "He *what*!"

"Admitted he's not my father, that his wife Luz was not my mother."

"You've had your head in opium fumes to believe that," Lassiter said, wondering. "You only imagined he said it, maybe."

Juanito's face was drawn, gray eyes reflecting the strain of his ordeal. "I did try to believe they were my parents. But all along deep inside I felt there was something nobody ever told me. Even when I'd ask him right out, sometimes making a joke of it, he'd never admit anything. He'd mumble something about my height being inherited from a great-grandfather and Andalusians had light hair like mine . . . Oh, hell, it's too late now to talk about it."

"Talk, Juanito," Lassiter urged in a low voice, stepping close to rest a hand on the younger man's arm. Juanito stared down at the damp stain of whiskey on the floor of his small cell. Lassiter watched him in the dimness, having to admit that at times he had wondered himself about Juanito's heritage, the towering young blond from diminutive dark parents, the pale gray eyes. Mostly the eyes.

"Miguel's been the same as a father to you," Lassiter

pointed out. "It's no excuse to go on a drunk and murder a man."

"I didn't murder him. No matter what they claim. But I was drunk, damned drunk. I hoped I'd just go to sleep and never wake up after what my father . . . I mean what Miguel confessed."

"Confessed he wasn't your father, you mean," Lassiter said, sensing more.

"Confessed that he and some other men murdered my real parents."

Lassiter stared in disbelief. "I don't believe that."

"Ask him. After I'm dead, *ask* him!"

"Why would he murder your parents?"

"There'd been some horse thieves raiding the ranches. Miguel lost horses, so did the others. My parents were drifters, working their way west. A stolen horse, a blooded stallion was found in their possession. They denied they'd stolen the horse, said it was loose and they saved it from going over a cliff or something. I really don't remember how Miguel put it."

Lassiter recalled Elnora saying that she suspected Miguel married her partly because of a guilty conscience about something.

"Go on, Juanito," Lassiter prompted.

"Everybody thought my parents lied about the horse. They tried to get away. They were gunned down. Everybody was surprised to find a baby in their wagon, me. Miguel took me home to his wife to raise." Juanito's lips twisted bitterly. "At least they didn't hang my parents, which is usually the fate of horse thieves. They saved that for me, the son." Juanito beat a fist against the wall, skinning his knuckles.

"Keep that up and you'll break your hand."

Juanito's smile was ghastly. "They figure to break my neck . . . at dawn."

"The way you tell it, Miguel said there were others in on the killing. Who?"

"He didn't say. Only that all were dead or moved away but him and one other. I've put two and two together and have an idea who it is."

"Tell me."

"It would hurt somebody and wouldn't do a damn bit of good anyhow. Even if she never bothered to answer my letters. Or even tried to visit me here . . ." Juanito suddenly clamped his lips together and turned away.

"You're talking about Ryerson's daughter. Was he one of them?"

"That's all I'm going to say, Lassiter." Juanito's voice was cold.

"Why in hell didn't you tell this at your trial?"

"Again, it would hurt somebody. This time Miguel, and do no good anyway."

"I thought you hated him."

"I'm torn . . . halfway love . . . for what he's done for me all these years. Halfway hate for his hand in murdering my parents."

"Maybe they *did* steal horses . . . I know it's no excuse for killing them, but . . ."

"The real thieves were caught later, Miguel said. One of them confessed that a stallion got away from them."

Lassiter watched agony flicker in the light eyes, seeing the turmoil. "If what you tell me is true, I don't blame you for getting drunk. But you shouldn't have taken it out on Miles."

"I didn't kill him."

"Why are you so sure?" Lassiter probed.

It took a moment for Juanito to speak. When he did, his voice was so low, so troubled that Lassiter had to lean close in order not to miss a word. From outside came the sounds of distant laughter from one of the camps under the trees. Faint strumming of a guitar. A man was to die; a time for celebration.

"Toby called me a greaser. I followed him outside, intending to fight him . . . in the alley behind Hopnatcher's."

"And you were wearing a gun."

"But I didn't touch it, I know I didn't."

"They said you had a gun in your hand."

Juanito shook his head. "I was stupid drunk, staggering. I tried to hit Toby. He knocked me down. He laughed at me and started to walk away. A shot came from behind a shed. When I turned around to look, something cracked me over the head. I was out cold. When I came to my gun was near my hand, not in it. There was a crowd standing around. Toby Miles was dead."

"Didn't you tell them about getting hit over the head?"

"Sure I did. They said that after I shot Miles that I fell down, drunk, and hit my head on a rock."

"And you didn't kill him."

"Somebody else did."

"I heard there was a forty-five slug in his back. Same caliber as your gun. And one shot had been fired out of yours." Lassiter watched the play of emotions across the taut face. "How do you account for that, Juanito?"

"You wouldn't believe me."

"Talk, damn it," Lassiter urged in a hoarse whisper. He looked around. Clyde Morton was still down the hall, leaning against the wall, shotgun under his arm.

Juanito spoke of the day of the murder. Hopnatcher's

had been crowded. Juanito drank and then found an empty deal table, sat down, put his head on the table and fell asleep. He had a muddled impression of someone lifting his gun out of its holster and returning it later.

"Whoever it was must have fired a shot out of it somewhere outside," Juanito went on in a dead voice. "Nobody would pay much attention to a gunshot when there was so much hell-raising that Saturday payday."

"Any idea who'd frame you?"

Juanito shook his head. "I've insulted a lot of people when I was drunk. Enemies I've got."

"Why didn't you tell the jury that story?"

"I did. They laughed."

Lassiter recalled his earlier conversation with the sheriff. "Lambert claims the saloon swamper was a witness . . ."

"He's missing most of his brains."

"And the other witness was Chick Kelleray. I remember that son-of-a-bitch well. He still around here?"

"I've been locked up, Lassiter, I've seen nothing, heard nothing . . ."

Lassiter dropped a hand to his empty holster, swore softly. "First thing is to try and get you out of here."

Juanito said bitterly. "You think I'm afraid to die? I'm not. I'd rather hang than keep on living in the kind of a world where . . ."

"That's fool talk and keep your voice down," Lassiter said under his breath.

He wheeled, knowing he was about to embark on the gamble of his life. One misstep and would-be rescuer and prisoner alike would be blown to a bloody smear by the deputy's sawed-off shotgun.

Chapter Eight

Lassiter stepped to the door. "Clyde," he called, pressing his face against the bars. As Clyde Morton pushed himself away from the wall and started toward the cell, Lassiter turned his head and said in a loud and angry voice, "Juanito, you're an ungrateful bastard. I want no part of you!"

Clyde tucked his weapon under an arm and rattled the large key into the lock. He paused, saying, "Could've told you you was wastin' your time with him, Lassiter."

Clyde Morton stood there on the other side of the barred door, a grin pasted on his thin lips. A lock of brown hair curled from under his hat. Lassiter tensed. *Turn the key* Lassiter wanted to scream at him.

"You stayin' for the hangin', Lassiter?"

"Think I'd miss a chance like that?"

For Crissakes . . . turn . . . the . . . KEY!

It appeared to stick in the lock.

Clyde seemed to be enjoying the moment. As if keeping Lassiter penned up a little longer with the condemned was punishment for ignoring good advice about visiting such an ingrate.

Lassiter's patience was thinning rapidly. His palms were damp. He tried to appear nonchalant. He knew from experience that a sheriff had often been known to sacrifice the hide of his deputy, but seldom his own. He needed Sheriff Lambert . . . *here.*

It had only taken a few seconds, but it seemed like

an age before Clyde finally turned the key. The deputy stepped back so Lassiter could leave the cell. The door started to swing shut. Clyde reached out for the key, still in the lock, to turn it the moment the door was fully closed. Lassiter's right fist slammed against the deputy's jaw. At the same instant he jerked free the sawed-off shotgun from where it had been nestled under the arm.

Clyde Morton's knees started to buckle. His eyes were glassy, slightly crossed. His mouth opened, the cords in his neck strained as he gathered breath to scream a warning. Lassiter caught him by an arm, slammed him against the cell door. Twin muzzles of his own shotgun dug into softness above the large brass buckle of his belt.

"Call the sheriff," Lassiter ordered in a low voice. "I want him . . . alone." And when the deputy's eyes began to clear, Lassiter added, "Believe me, Clyde, your life depends on it."

Morton paled. He raised his voice and did as he was told. "Tod! I . . ." He faltered. Lassiter dug harder with the shotgun, a strong brown finger hooked over the forward trigger of the weapon. A double blast from those barrels would cut Morton as neatly in two as if he'd been halved by a surgeon's knife. With the hubbub of voices in the office the sheriff hadn't heard him. Clyde tried again, louder. "Hey, Tod . . . Got somethin' to show you. Better . . . better come alone."

It hung in the air with a faint suggestion that something might be amiss in the cell that could embarrass the sheriff.

"'Scuse me, boys," Lassiter heard the sheriff say. There was the scrape of a kicked back chair. A sound of Lambert's boots thumping on the stone floor. The wall lamp had not yet been lighted. Lassiter held his breath. Clyde Morton sagged in Lassiter's firm grip that had shifted to the collar of his shirt, tearing it slightly. Through the bars Lassiter could see that faint color had returned to Juanito's face and there seemed a shred of hope in the eyes. Juanito stood stiffly in the white shirt and black pants the county had furnished for his execution. Voices had resumed in the office; a man laughed.

Sheriff Tod Lambert made the right angle turn from the office and came down the hall, arms swinging, big gun jiggling at his hip. "What you want, Clyde . . ."

He came up short when he saw the shotgun pointed at his belly.

"Over here, Sheriff," Lassiter ordered softly. "Walk easy and keep your mouth shut."

For a moment the sheriff's eyes turned ugly, then slid into fear when he took another look at the shotgun. He came forward a few steps, the round face taut with a combination of fury and apprehension.

"Lassiter, you're a plain stupid fool. All I got to do is open my mouth an' yell . . ."

"Do that and your head'll be raw meat."

"You ain't got the chance of a mouse in a box of torn cats gettin' that prisoner outa here."

"I don't believe he's guilty."

"Law says he is."

"With the hangman waiting, there isn't time to argue it out, Sheriff. That's why I'm taking Juanito. You're going with us. If you want to see the sun rise in the morning, you'll come along peaceable. Otherwise . . ."

Juanito's voice was shaking as he stepped from the cell. "My god, do you think we can do it?"

Lassiter said, "Take the sheriff's gun. You've got a right to defend yourself."

Lambert swallowed. "You'll get twenty years for

bustin' him outa here, Lassiter. He'll hang anyway. An' if anybody gets killed in this dirty business, you'll be right there on the gallows with him."

"When we git to the street, Tod, we'll fix him," Clyde Morton squeaked.

Lassiter tromped down on a toe of Morton's boot. And as the deputy's body contracted at the pain, Lassiter crashed upward with a knee, catching the deputy in the groin. As Clyde bent double, the same knee crashed into the face. Nose and lips seemed to explode in a gout of blood. Clyde Morton collapsed, out cold.

"March, Sheriff," Lassiter ordered. "You tell anybody who wants to be a hero that he just might make it. But at the same time you'll be splattered from here to the livery barn." He jerked his head. "Come on, Juanito. Keep right beside me. Match me step for step."

"Hey, Tod, what you an' Clyde doin' back there, anyhow?" came a querulous voice from the office.

"It . . . it's all right, Buck," the sheriff called hoarsely, eyeing the shotgun and the cold mask of Lassiter's face. "Everything's all right!"

They turned the corner in the corridor. Three men were left at the table, in the lamplight; the hangman was gone. A poker game had started. There were cards and chips and a bottle on the table.

At the sight of Juanito, Charlie Ryerson's jaw fell. He looked suddenly ill.

Lassiter warned the men at the table. "Any one of you make a fool move, the sheriff's dead."

They all looked at the short-barreled shotgun jammed against the sheriff's back and believed him. They seemed frozen in their chairs.

Lassiter one-handed the shotgun, snatched his .44 from a corner of the table where the sheriff had placed it earlier. He holstered it, then hustled the sheriff to the street.

Beyond the business block the camp fires were brighter, sparks dancing higher into the trees. A dim new moon yellowed cloud fragments. Lassiter, the sheriff walking stiffly in front of him, moved along the street, Juanito keeping pace. They came to the gallows, now in deep shadow. Men gathered there stiffened when they realized what was happening. A woman up the block began screaming. A man shouted.

The hangman who had been regaling some of the males with anecdotes pertaining to his craft, said mournfully, "I work all afternoon in the goddamn heat on that trap door an' now . . ."

"Shut up, Henry!" the sheriff roared. "Your troubles ain't half what I got!"

There were other shouts. The sheriff raised his voice. "Don't mess in this, boys. He ain't gonna murder me, once him an' that greaser friend of his gets clear of town. Then we'll get the biggest posse this county's ever seen. We just might hang 'em where we find 'em, by god . . ."

"For a gent who risks getting forty holes in his bull hide," Lassiter said coldly, "you talk too much."

Some children who had been in exuberant after-supper play, came scampering across a field to see the excitement. Mothers screamed at them to come back, one hysterically. Lassiter experienced a chill; he didn't want kids mixing in this. Stray bullets had little regard for age.

Just when Lassiter thought he might make it, he suddenly saw Miguel and his wife in front of the hotel. The little Mexican wore no hat; his head was bandaged, one arm in a sling. His weight rested on a cane.

Miguel Aleman attired in what he had once told Lassiter was to be "my burying suit." Elnora also wore black, hat and veil, the dress curved in at the waist to emphasize bosom and hips. Even now, Lassiter thought, you have to let every male know you're young and desirable.

Miguel stiffened as he realized what the somber parade down the walk meant, the corpulent sheriff, face almost a sunset scarlet in the wash of lamps in front of a store. Lassiter with a double-barreled shotgun. Juanito walking tall, pistol in hand.

Miguel started to reach for something under his coat, cane clattering to the walk in the abrupt stillness. Lassiter shouted a warning.

"Miguel, keep out of it!" And Lassiter knew that if his friend failed to heed the warning, somebody in the excited crowd might shoot him dead in the warped reasoning that the father was equally guilty as the condemned son. Or was Miguel reaching for a gun in a misplaced sense of justice, believing that his son could eventually be cleared in a court of law?

Not while the hangman waits not twenty feet away, Lassiter wanted to yell at him. He was relieved when Elnora placed a restraining hand on her husband's arm and spoke urgently. Although Lassiter could not make out what was said in that handful of seconds, he did know she echoed his own warning.

Some of the men along the street had recovered from their initial shock and were beginning to shout again at Lassiter and the prisoner he had freed, shaking their fists. A woman began to scream for her children to get away from potential danger.

Lassiter felt a drop of stinging sweat roll into an eye corner. He blinked it away, not taking a hand from the cocked shotgun aimed at the sheriff's broad back.

Patches of perspiration formed asterisks on the sheriff's faded shirt.

"Jump the bastards!" somebody yelled drunkenly.

And as there were added cries of assent, the sheriff's voice boomed louder and more authoritative; after all, it was his life on the edge, not theirs.

"Hold it!" he shouted. "Just everybody keep calm. We'll get 'em later." But Lassiter noticed that some of Lambert's bravado was veneer. The voice was hoarse with strain.

Lassiter swung them toward a hitch rack, his keen eye running along the line of animals tethered there. It would waste time going another block to the livery barn for his own mount. It was unsaddled, these at the rack were ready to run. He selected the ones he wanted, then gave Juanito a low-voiced order.

"You take the sorrel. Sheriff will ride the bay. I'll take the roan."

Lassiter then ordered everyone to stay back, and they did, staring open-mouthed, the children quiet at last, impressed by the peril of their sheriff. Lassiter told Juanito to mount up first, then keep the sheriff covered until he, Lassiter, reached the saddle.

"Hey, that's my hoss!" a man yelled, running from a saloon, wide hat brim flopping at each bounding step.

"Stay back, Ordway!" bellowed the sheriff. "You'll get your roan back, along with Lassiter's hide!"

"Hell with that . . ."

"Do what I tell you, goddamnit!" The sheriff's voice cracked. Others near the roan owner pulled him to a halt. He struggled, cursing, but they gripped him by the arms.

"Lassiter'll blow the sheriff right outa that saddle," one of them said loudly, "if anything goes wrong."

A swaying, drunken young man, no more than

sixteen or so, a lock of thick reddish hair hanging in his eyes, sounded aggrieved when he said, "Ain't never seen a hangin'. Was countin' on this one."

"You'll get your wish!" the sheriff said angrily; being on the back of a horse had restored some of his confidence.

"You try to put that animal in a run," Lassiter warned him, "and they'll have to pick up what's left of you with a mop."

And to forestall any such reckless move, should the sheriff be fool enough to try one, Lassiter snatched the reins away from him, brandishing the sawed-off shotgun in one hand.

"All I need is my finger, on the front trigger," Lassiter reminded. They were moving out, Juanito in the lead, then the sheriff and behind him Lassiter. Even if some hothead shot him in the back, the sheriff was a goner anyway; the shotgun would blow out his spine.

"Listen to me . . . *everybody!*" Lassiter shouted; he didn't need to get their attention. That he had already. Every pair of eyes on the street was riveted on the tall sinewy figure in the saddle, his horse and the sheriffs reined in close. The lethal Greener no more than a few inches from Sheriff Lambert's rib cage.

He warned the crowd not to try and follow them out of town.

Lassiter's mouth was dry until they were past the last alley and all that lay ahead was open country with a deeper shadow of hills and distant mountains faintly touched by moonlight. He gave the sheriff back the reins to his horse. Then he whacked the bay on the rump with the flat of a hand. The animal leaped ahead, Lassiter pounding close behind on the roan.

He yelled at Juanito in the lead; Juanito looked back.

Lassiter could see the whites of wide eyes, the pale blob of hair in the early darkness.

"If Lambert tries to get away, shoot him!"

"I'll shoot his horse instead," was Juanito's shouted reply.

Lassiter frowned. Wind stung his eyes as their mounts raced through the evening. "Not very bloodthirsty, are you?" But his words were lost in the rumble of hoofs. He looked back. Lamplit streets and windows were receding rapidly. He tried to detect signs of pursuit but saw nothing. He gambled that no one would try and close in on them because of the threat to their sheriff. Lambert might be a pompous, overfed politician, but everyone seemed to like him.

Even so, there was always the chance that some young fool, seeking to impress a female, might choose this occasion to prove himself heroic in her eyes.

When they slowed their horses on a grade, Juanito said, "I heard you say I wasn't bloodthirsty. I don't mind shooting the sheriff. I just don't feel like wasting a good bullet on him. I'd rather use my fists. He used his on me. Plenty."

Sheriff Lambert, hunched in the saddle of the sweated bay, growled something Lassiter couldn't make out. He didn't much give a damn. Again he pushed them to a gallop, driving the sheriff ahead of him. The range of dark hills was closer. They were through the first of the hills when Lassiter realized something was wrong. In the few seconds Lassiter had had to choose his horses, he'd hit two out of three. It was apparent now that the animal ridden by the sheriff was coming up lame. The horse slowed and was favoring its right foreleg. Lassiter nearly bumped into it with his roan.

He called a halt at a promontory and scanned their backtrail. Distantly in the clear air could be seen the yellowish blob that marked the site of Brightwater. Their dust hung in the incline they had just climbed. But there seemed to be no sign of pursuit.

"I had a hunch the real murderer was in town for the hanging and might trail us," Lassiter mused as he stood beside the sweated roan.

"The real murderer is right here. Him!" Lambert jerked a thumb at Juanito.

"Why would the killer want to follow us?" Juanito asked Lassiter in a dull voice.

"To silence you, maybe. Thinking you might come up with something you didn't remember at the trial."

Juanito's bitter laugh came out of the darkness. "I got damn little chance to talk at my trial."

Lassiter strained his ears, his eyes against the night for sight or sound of horses. He knew that by daylight they could expect company.

The sheriff was still making his threats, but grumbling them now in a lower voice.

When they were riding again, he said, "What I can't figure out is what's in it for you, Lassiter. I hear you never get mixed up in anything unless there's money in it."

"You wouldn't understand." Lassiter snarled it. He couldn't understand it himself.

"Miguel Aleman's no rich man, or is he? Seems that there ain't near the business at his place that there used to be."

"Miguel's not paying me. Now shut up about it."

"Or mebby it's that good-lookin' young wife of his who's gonna pay you in her own way . . ."

"Lambert, don't tempt me to break your teeth with a .44 slug."

The sheriff had started to laugh in a male, knowing way, but it faded quickly. He remained silent until they were deep in towering pines, and Lassiter ordered him to dismount. Sheriff Lambert protested in a tight voice when neither Lassiter nor Juanito stepped down. Lassiter picked up the reins of the lame bay the sheriff had been riding.

"You can't leave me afoot," Lambert said angrily, realizing Lassiter's intention.

"You are afoot and be glad you're still alive," Lassiter said. "Come daylight your friends from town will pick up our trail. They'll find you."

"Goddamn you, Lassiter, I'll remember this as long as I live."

"Shouldn't wonder," Lassiter said, reining the sheriff's horse in close so as to lead it easier.

"At least leave me my gun."

Lassiter gave him a hard smile. "So you can drill me in the back when I ride away?"

"Give you my word I won't."

"Think I'm fool enough to take it?" Lassiter turned the reins of the sheriff's horse over to a sullen Juanito. "Maybe I better have both hands free. Just in case our fat friend here figures to cave in the back of my head with a rock."

"I need a gun, damn it," the sheriff pleaded. "What if I get a mountain lion to deal with?"

"They'll never attack. Not unless they're starving."

"One of 'em might be."

"Then talk him out of eating you. Juanito, get moving!"

"I'm supposed to take your orders from now on?" the younger man asked with thin anger. "Hell . . ."

"I saved your neck."

"That automatically appoints you my guardian?"

"You're an ungrateful bastard."

The sheriff's bark of laughter followed them as they moved out. "I could've told you that you was wastin' your time with that no-good. He'll hang anyhow."

"Maybe not," Lassiter said over his shoulder.

"And you, my tough friend, will get those twenty years for your part in this business." Lambert shook his fist. "I'll see you serve them twenty years in Yuma Prison. *Yuma!* You hear me, Lassiter?"

Lassiter made no reply; he could barely make out the last of it, anyway, for their horses were scrambling up loose shale toward the top of a ridge. Soon they were dropping down on the far side on a long trail that twisted through shadowed trees. Clouds moved in for a time and the air smelled of rain. It grew darker than the inside of a sheepherder's boot, was the way Lassiter put it to Juanito. Then the moon broke through the clouds and they no longer had to grope their way downslope.

"Sorry for talking to you the way I did," Juanito said when they reached a flat section where they could be abreast, the limping riderless horse between them. "Truth is, I'm scared white." Juanito began to laugh, bordering on hysteria.

Lassiter was annoyed; he was letting down after all the tension involved in the jail break. "You find this amusing? I don't."

"I'm laughing at what I said. 'Scared white.' Hell, I *am* Anglo as my parents were, not Mexican." The laughter broke off abruptly and he added in a dead voice, "Suspected horse thieves, slaughtered without giving them a chance."

"*You're* getting another chance. Maybe in a way that makes up for it."

"Thanks to you. Took plenty of guts for you to face

up to that town the way you did. No denying that, Lassiter."

"A lot of it was pure luck. Getting hold of that shotgun was most of it."

"You could have done it even without the shotgun."

"Maybe. But there'd have been more risk in trying to convince that bunch to stay out of it." Lassiter stared ahead into the darkness, thinking. "There's something about a sawed-off shotgun that puts more fear in a man than anything else."

"I had a good example of it tonight."

After another hour, Lassiter reined in. They had some talking to do. . . .

Chapter Nine

"This is our first chance to talk," Lassiter said, "without Lambert overhearing something we don't want him to hear. Tell me everything you remember about that day . . . the day they say you murdered Toby Miles."

"I already told you."

"Tell me again, damn it. *Everything.*"

"You doing this because we're blood brothers?"

"Don't remind me of that! How the hell do I know why I'm doing it? Now will you talk?"

Hesitantly Juanito related events of a tragic day, the same day Miguel had reluctantly revealed the story of drifters, the doomed man and woman.

"I stole a bottle and rode for town. It was a hot day, hot as hell. I went into Hopnatcher's. He wouldn't sell me another drink. I went over to an empty table and fell asleep. I woke up with Toby Miles baiting me, saying I was likely more Indian than Mexican because no Indian could hold his whiskey any better than I could. I told him that was a lie because I had no Indian blood in me. But plenty of Mexican, he shot back. That's when I blurted out that I wasn't Mexican at all. He laughed and called me a greaser. Well, he said all Mexicans were yellow . . ." Juanito broke off and stared at the ground; their horses stood spraddle-legged a few feet away. There was a scent of pine and sage and dead ashes in the night air.

"Then what happened?"

"There was a lot of shouting back and forth. I was

worked up. Next thing I knew we were outside and he was knocking me down. I was so drunk I could hardly get my hands up. He beat me pretty thoroughly. He left me lying there in the alley. The few people who had come out to watch me try and fight him went back into the saloon. Toby Miles said he was pushing on . . ."

"Go on," Lassiter urged.

"I just remembered something. Toby Miles said, 'Chick's right, you are a yellow dog greaser.'"

"Chick . . . Chick Kelleray."

Juanito nodded. "Then Miles turned his back and walked away. There was a gunshot and he fell dead."

"That's when somebody hit you over the head," Lassiter prompted, "so you told me at the jail."

"Yeah. Like I said, I feel that someone got my gun away from me while I was sleeping at the table. Took it outside and fired it, then slipped it back in my holster."

"Chick Kelleray was one of the witnesses. And he's the one riled up Toby Miles to bait you. Bet a dollar I'm right."

"Kelleray, by god!" Juanito sounded excited. "He had an eye on Maggie Ryerson. And he didn't like it that I was her favorite . . . then . . ." The voice fell.

"What do you mean, then?"

"She turned against me, just like everybody else. Five times I wrote her from jail, but she never answered. Not one letter." Juanito was bitter. "A lot of people claim she's an uppity bitch. Maybe so."

Lassiter was inclined to agree. He made no comment. They had been riding again, heading south now instead of east.

They rode, made another mile or so, and saw a dim wash of yellow light. At the foot of the hill they were descending Lassiter could make out the dim outline of a small house, a barn and corral. Lassiter rode ahead, leading the sheriff's horse, Juanito hanging back. A dog began to bark. Lassiter tied the bay horse to a corral post; better than letting it wander loose and perhaps get hung up in thick brush.

A man shouted from the house. "Who's out there?"

But by the time the door was flung open, Lassiter and his fugitive companion were gone.

An hour later the cloud cover deepened. They stopped to water their horses at a creek. A breeze had come up, stirring an archway of cottonwood branches overhead.

Lassiter was in a foul mood, letdown from the hazardous night. And the fact that for the past few minutes Juanito had been arguing. He wanted to take over and try to clear his own name. Lassiter said he didn't have the experience for such a dangerous game.

"I'm going to talk to Chick Kelleray, if I can find him," Lassiter said flatly. "You're to stay out of it."

"Giving orders again?"

Lassiter made an effort to ignore him. "And I'll have a talk with Maggie Ryerson," he continued.

"I don't want you to talk to her."

"I'll do as I damn please," Lassiter said sharply.

"I'm *asking* you. Stay away from her!"

Lassiter emptied his pockets of all but an octagonal fifty dollar gold piece which he kept for himself. He pressed the rest on Juanito, who was reluctant to take it at first. Lassiter insisted.

"Your only chance is to head for the border. Ride by night and sleep by day."

"I still think it's up to me to clear my own name . . ."

"I'm damned sick of arguing. After a few weeks in Mexico, you write Miguel and let him know where you are."

"Lassiter, I appreciate what you've done. But I've got to run my own life."

"Great job you've done so far."

"Well, what if you'd been told that your parents had been murdered by the very man who'd raised you?"

"Other people in the world have had blows and learned to survive."

"Nobody you ever knew," Juanito said with a bitter laugh.

"Yeah, I did know one. A gunfighter turned lawman. He lost his right arm in a fight. But did he quit and feel sorry for himself?"

"Lassiter, you're beginning to sound like a preacher."

"This fella went into the mountains for six months and practiced and practiced till he got good with his left hand. Almost as fast with his left as he'd been with his right. Almost."

"Than what happened?" Juanito asked curiously.

"He was a mite slow, after all. But he tried. That's the main thing. As you've got to try."

Juanito's teeth gleamed in the moonwash through the trees as the clouds thinned. "Your gunfighter friend got killed, didn't he? All his work for nothing. As I'll probably end up on the gallows after all." He sounded despondent.

"I guess Miguel never took the time to beat any horse sense into you."

"Don't you try, Lassiter."

"Listen, kid, you're a wanted man. They'll shoot you on sight. Or have you back in the death cell. And this time you'll be so well guarded it'd take the U.S. Cavalry to get you out."

Juanito thought it over, jingling the gold coins Lassiter had given him. He stood beside his borrowed sorrel, pale hair rumpled. There was a rip across the back of his white shirt.

Lassiter spoke of a rancho just across the border. "They're friends of mine. They'll hide you out. Mention my name. And tell them Refugio was your brother."

"He wasn't my brother . . . I know it now."

"Christ! I suppose you're going to shout to the world about your parents. And Miguel's part in the dirty business."

"Haven't made up my mind yet."

Lassiter was drawing a map in the dust, of the rancho across the border, putting in landmarks Juanito would encounter on the way.

Lassiter looked up, throwing aside the twig he had used to scratch in the dust. "Miguel raised you, don't forget. Fed you and put clothes on your back and gave you a roof over your head."

"And killed my parents."

"That's in the past, damnit." Lassiter gestured angrily. "You should keep your mouth shut about the past. But it's up to you." Lassiter picked up the reins, preparing to mount. "I'll get word to you in a few weeks. If I can clear you, then you'll be free to come home."

"Home," Juanito said bitterly.

"If not, then you'll have to go deeper into Mexico. You'll never be able to come back. I'll do my best for you."

"I'm thinking it's hopeless."

"One thing you could do for me. Forgive Miguel."

"And forgive Charlie Ryerson and forgive his daughter because she's of his blood . . ." Juanito's voice trailed away as he stared at Lassiter in the faint light.

"So Charlie Ryerson *was* one of those with Miguel the day they corraled your folks."

Juanito drew a deep sigh. "Miguel said so."

"And Charlie Ryerson was there at the jail . . ."

"He'd never miss a chance to see me . . . hang." Juanito laughed; it had the sound of a man in pain. "I used to wonder why he hated my guts. Maggie . . . Margaret and I had to meet on the sly. The only way we could manage. He said I was Mexican and it finally dawned on me that that was why he disliked me so intensely. Now I see that he hated me because of his conscience." Juanito spoke the last of it through his teeth. "I should kill the son-of-a-bitch."

"Easy, kid . . ."

"He calls *me* a murderer. He's one two times over. My parents. Him and Miguel and two other men."

"What other men?"

"One is dead and the other is somewhere in Oregon, so Miguel said."

"Hatred won't buy you a damn thing, kid, but a bad stomach."

He handed Juanito the shotgun. "It'll whittle the odds a little if they jump you."

The eastern sky was rosy; it was dawn. They were both thinking the same thing. Had it not been the guts of one man and a lot of blind luck, Juanito would at this hour be climbing the gallows steps.

"Ride for an hour or so, then hole up," Lassiter advised. "Push on after dark. You listening to me?"

"I'll get going."

They mounted up, not shaking hands. Juanito turned his horse south, in the direction of Mexico.

Twice that day, after parting company with Juanito, Lassiter saw mounted men. They didn't need to carry a banner advertising who they were hunting for. He knew that already. He only hoped Juanito would follow instructions.

Lassiter circled back. Clouds rolled in, darkening the sky. The only thing he had to go on was a name, Chick Kelleray. And maybe even that was a lead that could peter out like sandy hoofprints in a windstorm. After all, would Kelleray frame Juanito just because of jealousy over that nose-in-the-air Ryerson girl?

Hadn't the Trojan wars gone on for years, Lassiter reminded himself, just because one hombre stole the wife of another? Anything was possible when the dirty business centered on a seductive female.

Chapter Ten

In Hopnatcher's Saloon the rumors were thick as the tobacco smoke that hung like blue-gray fog among the rafters. Men were draped over the barlip, talking excitedly about the daring jailbreak up at the county seat. A party of U.S. Marshals was on the way south to join the hunt for the killer, Juan Aleman, and the man known only as Lassiter. Authorities blamed the jailbreak on the incompetence of the Banner County Sheriff. Another rumor had it that the Cavalry was moving into that part of the territory. Someone said he'd heard that the territorial governor was borrowing a company of Texas Rangers.

Charlie Ryerson lumbered into the saloon, muddied and angered. "Bastards got clear away," he answered the many questioners who ringed him. "Chased 'em half the night. Then I gave up. I hear they found the sheriff."

"Found him dead, I reckon," a man said as more men crowded around the rancher who had just finished the long ride from Brightwater.

"Found him alive," Ryerson admitted.

A barkeep set out Ryerson's private bottle.

Hopnatcher, wearing his green eyeshade, said, "When we first heard about it everybody claimed Lassiter would kill Lambert sure."

"Well, he didn't. Which surprised me, to tell the truth." Ryerson poured himself a drink. His hand shook. He was practically out on his feet. He'd ridden with the posse for a few hours, then headed back to the county seat for a little rest before heading south. "And with Lassiter's rep," he continued sourly, "I *am* surprised. He's one tough son-of-a-bitch. Nobody made a move when he came out of that cell with the Mex. 'Course Lassiter had a sawed-off shotgun. But even so . . ." Ryerson noticed Chick Kelleray down the bar, thumbs hooked in a shellbelt, hat on the back of his head, wearing that cocky grin. A grin Ryerson despised.

"Mr. Ryerson, you gonna put up a *re*-ward for Juanito Aleman?" Kelleray drawled. Everyone looked around.

Ryerson didn't bother to reply to Kelleray's question. He tossed off his drink and told everyone he was going home and sleep around the clock. Kelleray followed him outside.

"You sure oughta put up a *re*-ward."

Ryerson turned his head. "Bring him in and I'll pay a thousand dollars. But you'll never earn it. You're too lazy."

"Maybe I'd rather have a job again at XR as my *re*-ward."

Ryerson was about to put his foot in the stirrup of his weary horse. A flicker of warning caused him to place both feet on the ground. "Forty dollars a month instead of a thousand in cash? Why?"

"You could make me segundo. One step short of bein' foreman. That could come a little later." Kelleray leaned close, that smirk pasted on his lips. "When I'm in the family, that is."

"I'll have some of my men take a sledgehammer to your kneecaps. You'll never walk again without crutches."

"I wouldn't do that, *sir*."

Ryerson narrowed his eyes. "You threatening me?"

"You murdered a couple of settlers some years back. How's that gonna set with folks around here who figure you're second cousin to God."

Ryerson felt as if someone had kicked him in the stomach. "Where'd you hear such a damned lie as that?"

"From somebody who overheard Miguel Aleman tellin' his kid about it. And your part in it."

"Overheard?" Ryerson's throat dried but he kept his voice steady. "Who are you talking about?"

"Never mind that."

"You better walk damn careful, Kelleray. You fool with me and you'll wish to hell *all* you had to worry about was being crippled."

"You can fix it with your daughter to marry with me."

"Why, you . . ." Ryerson's hand brushed the hell plates of a revolver under his coat. But when Kelleray's expression did not shift from cockiness to fear, his hand froze. "Just what is it you want, Kelleray?"

"I've done purty good by you so far."

"How do you mean that?"

"Juanito would've been hung by now if it hadn't been for Lassiter buttin' in."

Ryerson searched Kelleray's eyes, not liking what he saw. He decided to bluff. "Don't get in over your head in quicksand, Kelleray. You're already up to your ears."

Ryerson drew his gun, shoved the muzzle against Kelleray's throat. But the smirk did not vanish from the lips. "If you think you can make me squirm because of some imagined killings years ago," Ryerson snapped, "I'll . . ."

"Imagined?"

"If Miguel Aleman's been telling these lies, then I'll deny it to his face. Just who do you think people will believe? Me? Or that Mexican?"

"Miguel Aleman ain't the one I heard it from."

"Oh, yes, the person you say overheard such nonsense." Ryerson removed the gun from Kelleray's throat but did not put it away. "Then who did tell you that lie? I demand an answer."

"Let's just go along like I said. If I bring in Juanito you'll make me segundo . . . for now. We can talk about the rest of it later."

"Kelleray, you're on dangerous ground."

"No, you are. I hear you got plans, big political plans. You don't want anything to happen that might change 'em." Kelleray held the man's gaze. Finally Ryerson lowered his eyes and returned his gun to its shoulder holster. What he wanted more than anything was a good marriage for his daughter. It did not include Juanito Aleman. Certainly not this smirking lout now standing before him at the edge of the almost deserted street.

Ryerson took a moment to make sure his voice was steady. "You deliver Juanito to the gallows and we'll decide what to do next. Now get along and earn your money. Meanwhile, keep your mouth shut. *Shut!*"

Kelleray nodded, lifted a hand. "Adios," and slouched away.

Ryerson had already made up his mind to kill him eventually or better yet, pay someone else to do it. He thought of Lassiter who had been so deadly cool when he walked out of the county jail with a condemned prisoner. Lassiter, that was his answer, providing the man didn't skip the country for his part in the jailbreak. But if the man didn't skip, he'd hire him. When it was over, something could conveniently happen to Lassiter.

Kelleray rode south with two companions. Ray Parkinson's long face was mostly jaw. His right cheek was scarred and a finger was missing from his left hand. "How'd you make out with Ryerson?" Parkinson wanted to know.

"He's scared half out of his wits," Kelleray laughed.

"What the hell did you say to him to get him scared?" Joe Sawbridge asked. He was chunky, thin-lipped. During last roundup Kelleray had managed to get them hired on at XR as extras, but had lost his own job before he could contrive some way to make it permanent. They had grown up together in Abilene. Parkinson had spent a year in a Missouri jail for beating a woman nearly to death. Sawbridge was wanted in California for attempted murder.

"I know for a fact," Kelleray said, ignoring the other man's question, "that Ryerson wants to be named territorial governor so bad he aches just thinkin' about it. He sure don't want nothin' to wreck his chances." Kelleray winked at his companions, adding, "Such as an old murder."

Both men, riding with reins loose, looked surprised. Kelleray hadn't confided in either of them and they wanted to know what he meant about murder.

"You'll likely know all about it soon enough," Kelleray said. "First thing is to drag Juanito Aleman back to the gallows."

"Posse couldn't find him," Sawbridge grumbled, "how can we?"

"Got a hunch where he might go," said Kelleray. "To his pa's good-lookin' wife. Makes a man itch just to be away from her for an hour."

"An' you itch, I s'pose?" Parkinson muttered, not liking it that Kelleray chose to keep them in the dark.

"I learned a lot from that little lady." Kelleray gave them a wise look.

"You always was a hand with the gals," Sawbridge had to admit.

"Once I set my sights on one, she sure as hell never gets away." Kelleray's gaze darkened as he thought of Charlie Ryerson's uppity daughter. Turning him down for that goddamn Mex. Well, not exactly a Mex, as it turned out. If Elnora Aleman could be believed, that is. And he believed her. Because repeating what she had told him in a moment of weakness, then regretting it, had turned a tough old coot like Charlie Ryerson the color of bleached out canvas.

Soon as he got the chance he'd get off another letter to his brother Ed up in Colorado. The pickings down here were good, much better than a boring job as shotgun guard on a railroad. Here there was not only XR ranch but Aleman's Barn, each with a good-looking female that went with the properties. Ed would be eager for a change of scenery. Ed would be proud of him for getting everything set up. Usually it was Ed who had to do all the planning.

The only thing that had gone wrong was Lassiter. Kelleray and Ed had lost two of their shirttail kin when something went wrong. Only Freddie Peal had survived to carry the word to Ed that Lassiter hadn't been stopped. Kelleray had just received the letter general delivery that morning at Kendall Springs. Too late to stop Lassiter, even if it could be done.

It still had to be done. Parkinson he could count on, but he didn't know about Joe Sawbridge. Sawbridge didn't believe in a showdown unless the odds were one hundred per cent in his favor. "I stayed alive this long," Sawbridge was fond of saying, "'cause I know when to run and when to stand and fight."

In the deadly game Kelleray had decided to play, there was no room for Sawbridge's philosophy. If they didn't play their cards right in this one they were all dead.

They had no sooner reached the shack where they had been living off and on for the past week, than it began to rain.

Kelleray mentioned the letter he would write his brother Ed, his half-brother, really, but gave no details to his two shivering companions. The temperature had lowered by twenty degrees, the roof leaked.

"Ain't never seen two brothers closer'n you an' Ed," Sawbridge said.

Parkinson grunted. "My brother I hate. But you're right about Chick an' Ed. Closer'n laces in a miner's boot, Ed used to say."

Kelleray cleaned and oiled his guns. What he'd give if Lassiter would walk in the door. It was Lassiter who had come close to spoiling the game that Kelleray had engineered so carefully.

Chapter Eleven

Ned Hopnatcher was just closing up his saloon when he realized a side door was still unlocked. Most of the lamps were out but he could see a shadowy figure at the end of the bar. "I'm through for the night, friend. Sorry."

He ambled over to the side door and held it open, inviting the shadowy figure out.

The man spoke. "I need some information."

The saloonman's jaw dropped as he recognized the voice. "Lassiter!"

"I'm not going to hurt you. I'm trying to save a man's life." In his brief contacts with the saloonman, Lassiter had found him honest, compassionate. But he was realist enough to know that one could not always rely on externals.

"You're talking about Aleman's son." Hopnatcher wore his cracked green eyeshade. He removed it and carefully put it on the bartop. "I heard what you did up at Brightwater last night. Took nerve."

"Don't reach for a gun behind your bar."

"Don't figure to." Hopnatcher got out a bottle of good whiskey and poured each of them a drink. Lassiter dashed his off. It was what he needed. A rainstorm had drenched him. He was muddied, tense and close to exhaustion, but alert. He went over and locked the side door, turned down the wick of the remaining lamp so that he and Hopnatcher stood in deeper shadow. The town was asleep but there was no use in taking chances. Lassiter had been in the saddle most of the day, with little food, trying to get a line on his quarry. Having no luck, he decided to gamble on Hopnatcher, who had sent his bartender home and was working on his books at the bar. Lassiter waited until he was ready to close up.

Lassiter said, "Tell me about Chick Kelleray. I've got a hunch he's the one killed Toby Miles. Not Juanito."

"Jesus Christ!" Hopnatcher sputtered into his glass of whiskey. "You mean that?"

"Tell me about him."

"Kelleray's no good. Was surprised Ryerson kept him on as long as he did. But that's Ryerson for you. Hires tough men, dares them to go the limit and when they do, kicks them out." Hopnatcher regarded Lassiter for a moment in the dim light. "If what you say is true, it's a terrible thing . . . to almost hang a man for a crime he didn't commit."

"I don't have much to go on," Lassiter admitted. "Did Kelleray ever make any threats against Juanito in here?"

Hopnatcher sighed. "Well, the Aleman boy did give me a lot of trouble, getting drunk and all. He didn't drink so much at first, but then all of a sudden he went kind of loco. Yeah, come to think of it, Kelleray did say that he'd get Juanito come hell or high water on account of the Ryerson girl. I do recollect him saying it more than once when he was full of whiskey. But I figured he was just shooting off his mouth. He's pretty good at it."

"Why didn't you speak up at the trial?"

"Hell, Juanito went outside with Miles and there was a gunshot. And Miles was . . . Jesus, I just happened to think of something. Kelleray was one of the witnesses."

"He probably got your swamper to say he also saw the shooting."

"I admit my swamper is a little short on brains and could be easily influenced, but . . ." Hopnatcher broke off, then said in a stronger voice, "I recollect Toby Miles saying that Kelleray owed him three hundred dollars on some horse trade. And I know Kelleray didn't have the money. Toby was no saint, but he was a human being and didn't deserve to die like he did. It seemed that Juanito killed him, so I didn't do much thinking on the subject till now."

"Where does Kelleray hang out?"

"In here a lot of the time. Come to think of it, I saw him ride south this afternoon."

"Was he alone?"

Hopnatcher told him about Sawbridge and Parkinson. "They worked for Ryerson when Kelleray was there. Then they got to hanging around with the Monagals. Damn cow thieves, the Monagals. Hell, everybody knows it. Come to think of it, I haven't seen them for a spell. Bert and his boy Con used to come in here regularly. Tell you something else I've overheard Kelleray say in here."

"Tell me."

"He's got a shine on for Miguel Aleman's wife. You ask me, Kelleray might be heading in that direction."

Elnora and her hip-swinging walk flashed across Lassiter's mind. He gave Hopnatcher a hard look, dropped a hand to his gun. "I've got nothing to lose in this, Hopnatcher. I hope you'll keep quiet about me talking to you."

"You've got my word. Never had any use for Chick Kelleray. And Miguel's been my friend for years. If you can save his boy, I sure won't stand in your way."

Lassiter let himself out the side door. He wasted no

time in getting out of town. The saloonman seemed sincere, but Lassiter had sampled the world long enough to know that a knife in the back was sometimes delivered with a smile.

He needed rest. Ten miles south of town he found a niche between towering boulders that offered some protection from a cold wind that had followed the rainstorm. He staked out the horse, then went to sleep.

He arrived at Aleman's Barn in mid-morning just as a wagon loaded with supplies was pulling out. He kept out of sight until they were gone; two men in the wagon, another pair on horseback. Probably from one of the ranches to the south.

Lassiter scouted the place carefully, to make sure there were no other customers. From behind the stockade with its barred gate he could hear a mule braying, a stirring of horses. At least there were no wagons or saddlers tied to the hitchrail in front of the building. Of course someone could be holed up inside, perhpas one of those present two nights ago when he had bluffed his way out of the county jail with a condemned prisoner and a sheriff as hostage. One truth the sheriff had uttered; if things didn't work out, Lassiter could easily earn that twenty years of prison time. He recalled the sheriff vowing it would be Yuma, the hellhole of U.S. prisons.

And to make his position even more hazardous, he was riding a stolen horse. He slipped inside the building. The store was empty as was the dining room. Elnora was in the small saloon just clearing beer bottles from the bar. She didn't seem particularly pleased to see him.

"Thought Miguel didn't want you working in the bar," Lassiter said, looking around.

Elnora seemed on edge. She spoke of a man and

woman and son they had hired to do the work. Elnora had caught them cheating. "I had to get rid of them. So somebody has to run things around here. It's me."

"Where's Miguel?"

"He is . . . ill."

"Yeah, I saw him when I broke Juanito out of jail. Didn't look like illness to me. Looked like he'd been in a fight."

Elnora placed the beer bottles in a wicker basket, not looking up.

"I remember Chick Kelleray being in here a couple of times. He been in since I left?"

"Several times. Why?"

"You talk to him?"

"Of course I talked to him. How could I serve him whiskey and not talk to him?"

"Miguel too . . . ill to take care of his customers?"

"Miguel has been under so much strain because of his son. And he's been threatened . . ."

"Kelleray the one who threatened Miguel, beat him up?"

Her eyes sparked angrily. "You think I'd talk to Kelleray if I thought he was the one? I'd feel like shooting him instead."

"Who did threaten him, then?"

"Miguel wouldn't tell me. But I found a note under the door one morning. It said for Miguel to keep his mouth shut. It was unsigned.

"You still have it?"

Elnora shook her head, the red-gold hair touched by early sunlight through a narrow window. "I gave it to Miguel. He burned it."

"Who beat him up?"

"All I know is he rode north one day. Some of the XR

cowhands brought him back in a wagon. Said they'd found him lying beside the road."

"What'd Miguel say?"

"He said that's the way it happened. But he won't say whether his horse threw him or whether he was beaten. I do know he's frightened." She gave a sigh of despair. "Maybe it's my fault . . . I've been bad for him."

"In what way?"

"I have a feeling that someone's threatened to harm me. If Miguel doesn't do as he's told. But I have no idea who or what it might be. Just a feeling."

"Just a feeling, eh?"

"You look tired, Lassiter. Are you hungry?"

Lassiter admitted it. This morning she wore her braided hair pinned up. Her dress was green with a lacy high collar. She looked much too prim to be tending bar in a frontier saloon. She put on an apron, went into the kitchen and cooked him a breakfast of eggs and steak.

"We appreciate the risk you ran, trying to help Juanito," she said, setting the platter of food on the table. "I hope he's worth it. He's brought so much misery to his father."

"His father?"

"Well . . ." She got a strange look on her face. "Yes, his father."

He sensed she knew the story about Juanito's parents. Had Miguel told her?

Elnora watched him pepper his three eggs, cut into the thick steak. "Why were you so interested in Kelleray?" she asked.

"I think he framed Juanito for murder."

Her hand flew to her mouth. She stood rigid for a

moment, then slumped to a chair across from him. "My god, are you sure?"

"I hear he's taken a shine to you."

Elnora flushed and looked down at her hands clasped at the table edge. It was several moments before she spoke. "He has a certain charm. I lived in Kansas when I was a girl. He was born there. We had things in common, I guess you could say. I . . . I sometimes get so hungry for talk."

Or hungry for something else from a man that Miguel can't give you, Lassiter thought angrily.

She lifted her head, the blue eyes unwavering on his. "I know what you're thinking. I can see it on your face."

His smile was hard.

"There's been no one but Miguel," she snapped. "Sick as he's been in the time since you left here, there has been *no* one else."

"Tell me more about Kelleray."

"Damn you, Lassiter, there is nothing to tell." Then she got herself under control, smoothed her dress. "He asked for a job here. He had already apologized for the way he had acted in here the day Ryerson fired him and afterward. Said he'd had too much to drink and that it didn't happen often."

"Charmed you right out of your shoes, did he?"

"No, he didn't. But I admit . . . well, one day I did unburden myself . . . foolishly, I guess, in light of your suspicions concerning the man."

"Unburdened yourself, how?" He felt he already knew, but wanted to hear her say it.

Elnora spoke haltingly, saying that shortly after Lassiter had left them she had overheard Miguel and Juanito arguing. "It was late one night and their voices were loud. Well, Miguel isn't Juanito's father . . ."

"You know the whole story?"

"I asked Miguel the next morning. He told me."

"And you told Kelleray."

"I was so . . . so wrought up I just got to talking. It literally poured out of me. He seemed a good listener and I . . . I just didn't seem able to stop talking."

"Talkative females," Lassiter said through his teeth.

"Usually I'd resent that. But this time I deserve it."

A faint sound came from the second floor. Lassiter saw her look of agitation, saw her glance around at the staircase. Then she leaped to her feet and hurried to the stove for the coffee pot. He eased his gun in its holster as she refilled his cup.

Then he said casually, "Who's upstairs?"

"Only Miguel . . ." She turned her back quickly and returned to the kitchen with the coffeepot.

"If your friend Kelleray's up there, he's dead."

"There is no one upstairs but Miguel."

"I'll go have a look."

She gasped as she saw his drawn gun. "Please, Lassiter . . ."

Lassiter narrowed his eyes. "Then I'll just go upstairs and see my old friend Miguel. Unless you've got something to hide."

"You don't like me, Lassiter, and I can say it goes double in my feelings for you!"

"No need to lose your temper." He got to his feet. "You're holding something back. What is it?"

"Miguel told me not to let anyone know . . ."

"Even me, I suppose."

"I assumed he meant *everyone* . . . "

He wanted to shout "Liar!" His mind was racing as he stepped to a side window that overlooked the wagon yard with its stockade where he had finally terminated the long-standing feud with the Monagals.

Tied to a wheel of the upended wagon where the younger Monagal had made his stand, was a weary, mud-splattered sorrel.

"Last time I saw that horse, Juanito was riding him," he said, lunging at Elnora and seizing her by an arm. "I wondered why you didn't ask me about Juanito, what had happened to him after I broke him out of jail. You already knew. He's upstairs."

"Miguel was so worried someone might find out . . ."

Lassiter released her arm, glaring. "Might as well paint a sign on the front of the building as to leave that horse here. Let the world know an escaped prisoner is hiding under this roof. Juanito is a young fool. So are you, for not letting me know right off."

He gave her an accusing look that she met with chin lifted. "Got a hunch why he came back," Lassiter snarled. "You."

Lassiter spun away, took the stairs two at a time. A white-faced Juanito met him in the hallway with a cocked revolver.

"It's you, Lassiter," he said numbly and holstered the weapon. "I . . . I heard voices and thought maybe . . ."

"You should be damn near to the border by now," Lassiter cut in angrily.

"It seemed so . . . foolish to keep on running . . ."

"Hell of a lot more foolish to come *here!*"

A slight figure appeared, in a bedroom doorway, Miguel using a cane, his face still showing bruises. A face nearly as pale as Juanito's, an overlay of grayness on the dark skin.

Miguel spoke hoarsely in Spanish. "Lassiter, I appreciate what you have done for Juanito, but a decision has been reached. I go to Mexico with him. I will not let him go alone. My wife and I . . ."

Juanito stared at him. "That's crazy and you know it!"

Miguel argued. Lassiter stepped between them. "Miguel, just what'll you do with Aleman's Barn? Ride off and leave it for somebody to steal?"

"I will burn it down. Then nobody can have it." His small mouth twisted bitterly. "Might be better that way because the place has brought so little happiness. My first wife went to an early grave. Worrying that what I and others had done to Juanito's parents would come out and I'd go to prison . . . or hang. Juanito said that he told you the story . . . everything."

"Hang. That's what'll happen to Juanito," Lassiter said roughly, "if he doesn't get moving!"

"Lassiter, I *had* to come back," Juanito cried.

"For some noble reason, no doubt," Lassiter said sarcastically.

"I had to tell Miguel how it was. He came to visit me at the jail, but I refused to see him. He couldn't understand that by then I just wanted to get it over with. At the time I was still numbed by what he had told me about my parents."

"A tragedy," Miguel muttered, shaking his head.

"I feel a little better toward him than I did, Lassiter," Juanito went on, "but I wanted him to understand. You see?"

"Yeah, I see, but you're also loco to run this risk."

"I want to go with my son . . ." Miguel's voice cracked. He put a hand to his eyes. "I still think of him as my son."

"No time for sentiment," Lassiter snapped.

Elnora spoke from the foot of the stairs. "Lassiter, can't you have a little compassion? They've both been through so much."

Lassiter spun around to look down the staircase at

the slim figure. The possibility had already crossed his mind that Juanito had returned not so much for Miguel but to see his stepmother once again.

He had to admit he was enough of a cynic to question her motives: a sensuous handsome female marrying an older man when a virile young male was under the same roof. Then he shrugged the idea aside, deciding once again to give them both the benefit of the doubt. For the present at least.

He grabbed Juanito by an arm. "We've got to get out of here. We'll get fresh horses, turn the other pair loose . . ."

Juanito pulled away. His eyes, reddened from lack of sleep, narrowed to slits against Lassiter's face. The eyes were not the only imprint left by his ordeal of arrest, trial and sentence of death. Lines had deepened at the corners of his mouth. There was a gaunt look about him. Some of the body weight had been drained from the tall, big-boned frame by the attrition of past weeks.

"You said you're going to try and clear my name," Juanito began.

"Let's not waste time talking about it!"

"I'm going to help you. After all, it is my neck."

"My neck, too. I don't fancy spending twenty years in Yuma Prison. Besides, you'll only be in the way . . ."

A sudden muted sound of horses reached them from the road. Riders! Lassiter strained his ears, hoping to hear signs that they were moving on, not stopping. The sounds grew louder, halting at the far end of the building. Elnora gave a low moan of fright, one hand clutched the banister. "Good Lord, it's the sheriff and some men," she called up to them.

Lassiter sprang to a window that overlooked the east-west. Below was Sheriff Lambert and five men, a weary, muddied group who looked as if they'd been caught in the same rainstorm as Lassiter. Lambert rattled the main door. It was locked.

"Try the saloon," Lassiter heard the sheriff say.

Elnora sped away on tiptoe to try and bar the saloon door on the inside. She was too late.

Miguel whispered, "I'll try and stall them. You and Juanito watch your chance and get away."

Miguel limped down the stairs, his cane thumping on the treads.

Lassiter heard Sheriff Lambert's booming voice. "That kid of yours, Miguel. You seen hide or hair of him?"

Miguel hesitated; Lassiter knew it hurt his pride to lie. "No, I have not seen him."

"Didn't figure he'd be fool enough to come here, anyhow. Lost his sign, picked it up again. Then damn if we didn't hit rain. Washed out the tracks of him an' that goddam Lassiter. Hadn't been for Lassiter, you'd be claimin' your son's body about now . . ."

"That's a cruel thing to say, Sheriff." Elnora's voice was strong, faintly patronizing. "And you certainly don't seem like a cruel person. In fact, this county is lucky to have a man of your stature as sheriff."

"That's poppycock." But from Lambert's tone, Lassiter knew he enjoyed being flattered by a charming female. "Your stepson . . . seems funny sayin' it that way, ma'am. You bein' almost as young as him. But he got away with my gun. It was a good one. I figure Aleman's Barn owes me."

"Of course. Anything you boys want to drink will help make up that payment," Elnora said cheerfully. Miguel agreed; and it was no time to quibble about lost profits. Juanito's life was at stake. Lassiter's freedom.

"Miguel, why don't you serve them what they want,"

Elnora said, her voice steady, "while I go and make them some meat sandwiches. They look starved."

This followed by a murmur of voices, a sound of bottles and glasses being thumped down on the bar. Lassiter and Juanito crept down the stairs, trying to keep out of the line of the open doors between bar and dining room. Elnora, white-faced, came out of the barroom.

She made a helpless gesture, standing wordlessly by one of the tables. Lassiter signaled her that it was all right, they were on their way. Purposely he had not tied his horse in front, but around the side so it could not be seen from either of the two roads, north and south and east and west.

"I'll have me this drink of whiskey," Sheriff Lambert was saying to Miguel, "then we'll take a look around. Just in case . . ."

By then Lassiter was quietly closing the heavy door that led to the yard with its wrecked wagons, barrels and odds and ends of junk. He gestured for Juanito to get his horse; it was still saddled and there was no time to get another. Lassiter reached his own mount. Elnora had begun to sing in a loud clear voice as she worked away at the stove.

"Bless her," Lassiter muttered.

"I didn't know she could sing," Juanito said, riding up.

"Maybe not the best voice in the world:" Lassiter was thinking of Bessie up in Denver. "But thank God it's good and loud."

They walked their horses to the west end of the building, away from the bar and dining room.

"That was a close one," Juanito said, shaking his head.

"Too close."

"Good thing you were there. I'd probably have panicked and run. And they'd have had me sure." It ended on a note of despair.

"This time when I say head for Mexico, do it!"

"I guess I can see now that my hanging around could jeopardize Miguel's life. And Elnora's. What a woman she is."

Lassiter glanced at him from under a tilted hatbrim. My blood brother, Lassiter thought, and wanted to laugh. And with all the risk he wasn't making even a centavo out of it.

Lassiter thought it best to circle north a mile or so and then swing east, using the hills as cover. He intended to see that Juanito got into the mountains and once again headed in the direction of the border. Once Juanito was off his hands, Lassiter intended to pick up Chick Kelleray's trail. He considered making Juanito swear an oath that this time he'd follow directions and not turn back, but keep on until reaching the sanctuary across the border. Then he decided that swearing oaths was for empty-headed fools like himself. He gave up the idea.

They had traveled less than a mile, keeping to a tree-lined creek, when a sudden flash of light caught Lassiter's attention. Lassiter held his breath, staring ahead at a slope of hill where he had seen the flash of light. When it came a second time he crowded Juanito's horse into a draw.

Chapter Twelve

"What is it?" Juanito demanded, his face losing color.

"Somebody with field glasses," Lassiter said, swearing under his breath. This was the distance for a rifle. He thought of his Winchester that he'd left in the hotel up at the county seat. He had intended picking a rifle out of the stock at the trading post but the sheriff's sudden appearance had negated that idea. Now all he had for distance shooting was his .44. Juanito didn't even have the sawed-off shotgun that had gotten them out of the Banner County Jail. Not that it had any distance, but the weapon would certainly narrow the odds if it was a posse ahead and they swarmed in on them. But Juanito had left the weapon back in his room.

"You stay here," Lassiter said, dismounting. He climbed to a rise of ground. From here, through a screen of thornbush, he could see a man on a ledge of rock that jutted from the side of a hill. The man held a pair of field glasses to his eyes, staring in the direction of Aleman's Barn. He appeared to be alone.

"Looks like your friend Kelleray," Lassiter called tensely over his shoulder. "But I can't be sure on account of the distance."

Juanito joined him, panting a little from the climb. He confirmed Lassiter's suspicion with a growled oath. "That's the son-of-a-bitch who framed me! I know it now, sure as I know there's blood in my veins!"

Lassiter looked around at him with faint surprise. Juanito had always seemed more or less passive, not given to violent outbursts; a sullen young man whom Lassiter had disliked. Therefore he wasn't prepared for the vehemence and Juanito's sudden move.

Before Lassiter could grab him, Juanito had flung himself back down the slope and into the saddle of the borrowed sorrel. Lassiter nearly reached him, his fingertips brushing a leg. But Juanito was spurring the horse plunging over the brushy lip. In his hand was the revolver appropriated from Sheriff Tod Lambert.

Lassiter tried to keep his voice down so as not to alert Kelleray on the lip of the flat rock, partially concealed by mesquite. Kelleray was still studying Aleman's Barn through the field glasses, but already stiffening at sounds of the horse.

"Juanito, for Christ's sake! Come back!"

By then Kelleray was fully aware of the horse coming at a dead run. Releasing the glasses which hung from a strap looped around his neck, he spun around. Instead of firing as Lassiter expected, Kelleray bounded from the rocky shelf and disappeared somewhere in thick brush behind a shoulder of hill.

And then as Lassiter leaped into the saddle, he heard Kelleray's triumphant shout. "Just like a stupid Mex to ride into a trap!"

And trap it was, for sure. Any gunshots would alert the sheriff and his five men and probably bring them at a gallop to see what was going on. Lassiter rode slowly, carefully.

Kelleray wasn't alone, for Lassiter could hear a second voice. "Hey, greaser, say hello to the hangman," this shouted mockingly.

"No hangman for this bastard!" Kelleray roared. "He goes back dead!"

A third voice, harsher than the others, but pitched lower. "Juanito ain't alone. Somebody with him, by god!"

It confirmed what Lassiter already suspected. He and Juanito had not been seen, not until the latter, blundering after Kelleray, had given their approach away. Lassiter ducked his mount back into the draw, trying to pick up other voices. But there seemed only the two men with Kelleray. Of course he couldn't be sure, he knew damn well, but there was no time to wonder about it. If Kelleray made good his threat, Juanito was as good as dead. And Lassiter knew they'd do their best to make sure he was next.

Disregarding the odds, Lassiter suddenly pushed his horse hard, thankful for the screening of giant boulders and heavy undergrowth at the base of steep hills. As he swung hard right, the horse stumbled. A rifle bullet whipped overhead. Lassiter literally hauled the horse back in stride with the reins. He'd never know for sure, but perhaps the faltering mount had saved his life.

His .44 was out, firing, a wink of muzzle flash bursting from the barrel where mesquite grew thick enough to cast long shadows. A man with a long-jawed face looked surprised. He was afoot and tipping toward the rifle that already was slipping from his fingers. A blue shirt faded almost white from many washings in lye soap, blossomed redly on the left side, high up on the chest.

Lassiter reined his horse hard left, praying it would this time keep its footing. A revolver crashed, the heavy sound of a .45. Something tugged at the crown of his hat. He put two blasts from his gun where he believed the man with the .45 might be hiding. He heard no howl of pain. He did hear, however, a sudden roar of hoofbeats, moving away at a gallop.

This followed by Kelleray's bellow of protest. "Joe . . . Sawbridge . . . where the hell you goin' . . ."

"He killed Ray! Ride for it, Chick, we'll get him later . . ." Sawbridge was yelling. "It's that goddamn Lassiter back there in the brush!" Joe Sawbridge burst into view, fifty yards to the north, bent over in the saddle, not looking back. He kept going, wind ballooning the back of a gray shirt from the fast pace set by his mustang. Lassiter did not waste a shot on him because of the distance but slowed his horse, standing up in the stirrups to try and locate Kelleray in boulders or the several draws at the foot of the hills. Powder smoke hung in the air like a blue veil.

A slug from Kelleray's gun slammed into mesquite above Lassiter's head, bringing down a shower of twigs.

"Mebby Sawbridge wants to run an' fight another day," Kelleray taunted, out of sight at the base of the hills, "but not me! You want to see your Mex friend alive, you throw down your gun an' come ahead with your hands . . ."

Lassiter swerved aside, his horse smashing brush. For the moment he was out of Kelleray's range of vision. Lassiter cut the stride of his mount so as to come in from the rear of the cul de sac that Juanito had blundered into so foolishly. He caught his first glimpse of Juanito, some forty yards away, lying on his side, legs drawn up, as if already dead. Lassiter's mouth dried as he thought of the great risks involved in the jail break and all the rest of it. For *nothing*? Nearby was the crumpled figure of the long-jawed rifleman Lassiter had shot. He was unmoving and no wonder. The .44 had shattered the crown of his balding head.

Kelleray was taunting him again. "Hey, Lassiter, show yourself, if you got the guts!"

Lassiter said nothing. He knew Kelleray was trying to goad him into speaking so as to have an idea where he might be in the maze of brush and boulders. Lassiter had already gauged the location of Kelleray by his voice. He suddenly sent the tired horse sweeping around a shoulder of rock. He saw Kelleray half turned, crouched beside a boulder, peering through the wall of mesquite as he tried to spot the enemy. However, he was looking in the wrong direction. But already he was reacting to the sudden burst of hoofbeats as Lassiter's horse surged to a hard run. Frantically he swung up his gun. Lassiter beat him to the first shot. But the bullet ricocheted off the field glasses dangling across the front of the shirt. Half of Kelleray's left ear disappeared, ripped off by the slug in wild, unpredictable upward flight. Kelleray screamed. His knees started to fold. Then he stiffened them, lifted his gun. No longer was there any trace of handsomeness left in the face. Fear was stamped in the eyes. Pain had erased the familiar smirk leaving instead lips that were pale and writhing in agony.

Not only pain from the shattered ear, but also no doubt from impact of the field glasses smashed against his chest by the force of the bullet.

Kelleray fired, missed. Lassiter tried for a leg shot, wanting him alive to climb the gallows that had been built for Juanito Aleman. But Kelleray managed to wheel aside, trying desperately to reach the far side of a boulder which would offer shelter. Lassiter spurred after him. Kelleray twisted around, dropped to one knee to steady his aim. Lassiter was bent over in the saddle, his horse at a hard run along the narrow slot where the hills folded together into towering rock and on either side almost impenetrable brush. Lassiter was aware of a bullet inches from a cheek. He reined in before Kelleray could snap off another shot. Lassiter tried again for a leg wound. But the wildly scrambling

Kelleray took the bullet instead just below the left armpit. It spun him around. He collapsed, moaning, his feet flying up as he fell heavily on his back. Lassiter bounded from the saddle and sprinted along the narrow clearing. Hoofbeats to the north were fading. Apparently the fleeing Joe Sawbridge had no intention of returning.

Lassiter slowed, glanced at Juanito lying on his side. He was heartened to see no grayness of approaching death visible on the face. And a faint stirring at the chest meant that he was still alive. At least that much luck for his blood brother.

Lassiter put his attention on the man he wanted. Kelleray had not moved. Lassiter disarmed him, reloaded his own weapon.

"Kelleray, can you get on your feet?" Lassiter demanded.

"Had everything perfect . . . Toby Miles . . . damn thief . . . figured to cheat me outa three hundred dollars . . . Juanito hung for it . . ." Kelleray rolled his eyes up to Lassiter hovering ominously above. "You had to horn in . . ."

"You're riding with me to Aleman's Barn. Sheriff's likely still there and by God you're going to tell him about that murder!"

"Christ, I'm hurting," Kelleray moaned, teeth clamped against spreading pain. Pallor began to wash out his sun-darkened features, accentuating the freckles. Kelleray was in no condition to sit a saddle, Lassiter could see that. In fact, he might not last to Aleman's Barn, even lashed to a horse.

Lassiter wondered how he could obtain a confession in writing, but he had no paper at hand, not even a pencil. Then he was aware of horses approaching the row of hills at a gallop, coming from the direction of

Aleman's Barn. It could very well be Sheriff Tod Lambert and his small posse, attracted by the gunfire that surely would have carried to the trading post in the clear air. He had confirmation of this when he parted the brush and saw the red-faced sheriff less than a hundred yards away, pounding toward the hills, his five men strung out behind.

Lassiter heard Juanito call his name in a weak voice. He looked around. Juanito was sitting up on the ground, a dazed look in his eyes. And no wonder. Lassiter saw an ugly gash at the temple that had probably been made by a gun barrel.

Lassiter gestured for him to stay put. "Don't move from there," he called hoarsely. "Your life depends on it."

Juanito's gaze began to clear when he saw Kelleray bleeding badly in Lassiter's grasp. "So you got him!"

"He's about to talk . . . talk loud and clear."

Kelleray bared his teeth. "Go to hell . . . both of you." Kelleray's voice acquired an edge as he seemed to realize his desperate position. He fumbled the battered field glasses from his neck, then tried to crawl toward a gun lying in the dust next to the body of Parkinson, whom Lassiter had killed. Lassiter booted it out of reach, then caught Kelleray by an arm and hauled him to his feet. The rough handling caused Kelleray to moan. He protested as Lassiter forced him to hobble up a slight incline to the lookout perch he had used to scan Aleman's Barn through field glasses.

Sheriff Lambert and his men had reined in below, the horses milling about. One of the possemen, lank and redbearded, shouted at the sheriff. "Shots come from over yonderly." He gestured eastward with a long arm.

Lambert, looking grim, shook his head. "We'll take

a look here first . . ." He broke off, an oath exploding from his lips as he glanced up and saw Lassiter appear on the rock shelf some fifteen feet above. Chick Kelleray sagged at his side. Lassiter's gun was rammed against Kelleray's rib cage.

The sheriff recovered. "Lassiter, you're under arrest . . ."

But Lassiter had other ideas. "Make a wrong move," Lassiter shouted down at him, "and Kelleray's dead. You'll never know the truth about murder . . . !"

"I *know* the truth about murder!" Lambert yelled.

"Kelleray's going to tell who killed that horse trader!"

Some of the men below seemed surprised, exchanged glances. Lambert was torn with frustration, rage, but still interested enough to lean his big body forward in the saddle to listen.

"Tell 'em, Kelleray!" Lassiter snarled. He knew it was a gamble. At any second one of the men below could start firing. Weak as he was, Kelleray tried to straighten up, but Lassiter held him rigidly in an awkward half-crouch.

"Won't say one damn word," he finally slurred.

"Sheriff, Kelleray's the one did it. Framed Juanito!"

Kelleray's legs gave way. Lassiter let him sink to his knees, but did not ease pressure of the gun. Blood darkened one side of Kelleray's shirt. With only parts of gristle and flesh of the missing ear still attached to the skull, he looked grotesque.

Sheriff Tod Lambert's hand rested tentatively on the butt of a booted rifle as he squinted up at Lassiter, who shouted at Kelleray.

"Talk, Kelleray, *talk!*"

The sheriff, on a nervous mount at the base of the hills, finally decided to free his rifle. "Turn Kelleray loose, Lassiter. You're under arrest . . . I won't say it again!"

Lassiter only tightened his grip on the man. "Kelleray, tell the straight of that murder. Talk, goddamn it! And, Sheriff, you better listen to what he's got to say."

"Why . . . the hell . . . should I?" Kelleray's voice lost strength and the sentence ended in a sob. Sunlight through the overcast, glinted on six rifle barrels below. Aleman's Barn was a dun-colored blob in the distance.

Lassiter knew Kelleray was weakening and shouted again. "You've got a choice. We'll see you get to a doctor. Or you can stay on this hill and bleed to death. Take your choice!"

"Toby Miles . . . the bastard . . . deserved to get a bullet in the back," Kelleray began, his voice faltering, apparently swayed at the hope of easing his pain. But only momentarily it seemed. Lambert and his men had quieted as Kelleray started to talk. They stared in fascination at the tableau on the jutting shelf of rock above.

Kelleray, dazed as he was from shock and loss of blood, noticed the change in the onlookers and tried to correct the mistake the loose tongue had produced. "Sheriff . . . don't listen to Lassiter. He . . . he killed the Monagals, sure as hell. I found their grave, but coyotes had got to it and there was only bones."

Lassiter wasn't surprised that Kelleray had brought up the Monagals to draw attention away from himself. He forced a scornful laugh while watching Lambert's upturned face from a corner of his eye. "Who the hell can identify bones?" Lassiter shouted. He shook Kelleray savagely. "You murdered Toby Miles!"

Kelleray sobbed. "You don't know what pain is . . ."

"Confess! Then you'll have a doctor!"

One of the possemen started to level his rifle, but the sheriff, apparently intrigued to a point, barked an order. "Hold it, Fred. You'll only get Kelleray killed. All Lassiter's got to do is drop the hammer of that pistol. Besides, let's hear what Kelleray has got to say."

Kelleray tried to pull away from Lassiter, but lacked the strength. Lassiter tightened his grip on the right arm. Kelleray's left was stained with blood from the shattered ear and from the bullet hole under the armpit.

Lassiter refused to let up on him, knowing that time was running out for them both. "You'll get laudanum to ease the pain. You'll have a doctor."

Sheriff Lambert waved two of his men over. They edged their horses in closer and listened to his whispered orders. Obviously they were to try and slip around behind the hill and take Lassiter from the rear; they started in that direction, walking their horses so as to be as inconspicuous as possible. Lassiter wasn't fooled. He knew that any second could bring disaster. He sweated as he tried again.

"Kelleray, speak up, or you'll bleed to death!"

Kelleray broke. "I killed him. I killed Toby Miles."

The sheriff's jaw fell; every face below was jolted by surprise.

"Details, Kelleray." Lassiter kept at him. The sheriff leaned forward in the saddle so as not to miss a word.

"Oh, gawd . . ." Kelleray moaned.

"How'd you frame Juanito Aleman?" Lassiter demanded.

For only another moment or so did Kelleray hold back. Then the promises of medical aid finally overrode his reluctance to confess. When he spoke, his voice was so low that even Lassiter could only hear half of what he said.

"Speak up! Louder. You can do it. Confess and you'll be out of your misery."

It spilled out of the man haltingly. He told how he had seen Juanito dead drunk in the saloon, asleep at a deal table. In the crowded room he had watched his chance and slipped Juanito's gun from its holster and gone outside with it. It was a Saturday, payday. Many cowhands in town, some shooting at tin cans in a nearby vacant lot. Kelleray fired one shot from Juanito's gun, then slipped back to the empty deal table where Juanito was still passed out. He returned the weapon to its holster. He waited a few minutes then contrived to get Juanito and the horse trader into a violent argument, triggered by references to the younger man's ancestry, the word "greaser" being injected into the exchange.

There had been a brief fist fight in the alley, Juanito easily knocked down. Onlookers returned to the saloon. Toby Miles started to walk away, intending to leave town for more horse trading. Kelleray shot him in the back, then hurried to the crowded saloon, shouting that Miles had been shot. He joined the others erupting out the alley door. They found the horse trader dead, Juanito just regaining consciousness. One shot had been fired from the gun laying near Juanito's hand. It was the same caliber slug as the one removed from the body of Toby Miles.

"Juanito claims somebody or something hit him on the back of the head," Lassiter prompted. "Tell us, Kelleray."

"I . . . throwed a chunk of 'dobe brick."

"Tell *why* you framed Juanito."

"Mostly because of Maggie Ryerson . . . but Toby claimed I owed three hundred . . . I never owed a cent . . . but mostly it was Maggie," he repeated with a sob.

During the confession, Lambert had dismounted and climbed, short of breath, to the rocky shelf.

"Kind of a mess, ain't it, Lassiter?" he panted, looking down at Kelleray crumpled on the rock slab. Then he shouted down at his men. "Two of you boys head back to Aleman's Barn and git a wagon. Kelleray's purty far gone for settin' a saddle."

And it was then that he noticed the slim rider sitting the saddle of a roan. Lambert seemed surprised to see Elnora Aleman, in riding clothes, hat on the back of red gold hair, staring up at him. Even Lassiter had not noticed her until that moment, everyone's eyes having been intent on the wounded man admitting to a murder.

"How long you been settin' there, Mrs. Aleman?" Lambert called to her.

"I heard everything," she replied coolly. And as if to make sure he understood, she repeated it. *"Everything."*

"Kinda looks like we got us a witness, don't it, Lassiter?" Lambert said, pulling at a lower lip.

"You mean your own boys weren't?" Lassiter said wryly.

Lambert squirmed, shot him a look. "Like I said a minute ago, it's kind of a mess. Charlie's a mite touchy these days an' he won't like it worth a damn his daughter's name bein' dragged into it. But reckon he'll have to live with it, eh?"

Elnora urged her mount forward. "Miguel isn't able to ride yet. When we heard the shooting and the sheriff went roaring off in this direction, I volunteered to see if . . . if everyone was all right." She looked directly up at Lassiter out of large blue eyes. "Juanito . . . is he alive?"

Lassiter nodded. "Why don't you ride back with the boys going for the wagon? Tell Miguel everything is all right." Then Lassiter straightened up; the sheriff had knelt and was using a bandanna as a compress to check the bleeding at Kelleray's side. There was nothing that could be done for what remained of the ear. "She can take that message to Miguel, can't she, Sheriff? That everything is all right?"

For a moment Lambert seemed to be weighing his reply. Then he said, "Reckon," without looking up.

Lassiter was satisfied. He gestured for Elnora to leave, but she seemed reluctant. When he waved an arm toward Aleman's Barn, she hurried to join the two men Lambert was sending for the wagon.

Down in the cul de sac, Juanito had gotten to his feet. He stood with fists clenched at his sides, a stricken look on his face as Lambert spotted him. Juanito seemed to be holding his breath. Spots of blood had dried on his neck and shirt from the savage blow he had taken at the temple.

Sheriff Lambert jiggled nervously from one foot to the other, then frowned. "By rights I oughta ride you an' Lassiter to the county jail. You two hombres stole some hosses."

"They're no worse for wear," Lassiter pointed out. "You can see that they get back to their owners."

Lambert chewed that over, plainly not liking it. Elnora Aleman being a witness had made his position restrictive. When Kelleray moaned again, Lambert looked down at him seated there on the rock shelf, one arm supporting his weight.

"I'd heard talk you was sweet on Maggie Ryerson," the sheriff said angrily. "But, Jesus, to frame a man for murder."

One of the riders a grizzled stocky man, spoke up, "Sure looks like you'll git to use them new gallows after all, Tod."

Lambert spoke crisply to Juanito, who still looked partially dazed. "Wa'al, mebby you learned a lesson outa all this, anyhow."

"He didn't *do* anything," Lassiter reminded. After tensions of the gunbattle and what followed, he was let down, angered that the corpulent sheriff found it a time to nit pick.

"Don't you go buttin' in, Lassiter." Sheriff Lambert's voice rose. "I ain't forgot how you made a fool of me in front of the whole town!"

"Better to hang an innocent man?"

Lambert stroked his heavy jaw between thumb and forefinger. "Wa'al, mebby not," he conceded. Then he leveled a finger at a shaken Juanito. "You was flyin' mighty high there for a spell. You see what can happen to a fella when he's got a quick temper an' too much forty rod under his belt."

"I'm through with whiskey," Juanito said in a dead voice.

"Let him be on his way, Sheriff," Lassiter urged. "He's got a bad cut on the head. His stepmother can tend to it."

"Yeah, go ahead," Lambert grunted. Kelleray had started to ramble.

"I figured it was a chance for me an' my brother Ed . . ."

"Chance for what?" the sheriff demanded, bending over the stricken Kelleray.

"Aleman's Barn . . . Juanito outa the way . . . get rid of the ol' Mex. Marry the good-lookin' widow . . ."

"You better keep shut an' save your strength," Lambert advised. "We'll have a wagon here directly."

Kelleray seemed not to hear him; his eyes were wide, glassy with fever. "We had the same ma but a different pa. But even so, we was . . . was closer'n . . . laces in a miner's boot, as Ed used to put it." Kelleray turned his face to the clearing sky. "Oh gawd, won't I ever see my brother again?"

Kelleray's arm supporting his body in a sitting position, suddenly buckled. He fell back, mouth open, eyes unblinking at the sun overhead.

Lambert muttered something, then felt of Kelleray's wrist instead of placing a hand over the heart for signs of life. That side of the shirt was soggy with blood.

"Looks like the boys'll be haulin' back another dead one." Lambert walked down the slant, through thick brush and to the first man Lassiter had killed. "Don't recollect this one's name, but he worked a spell for XR. Ryerson's foreman will remember him. But he changes foremen about like most fellas change their socks."

Lassiter mentioned the one who had fled. "Kelleray called him Sawbridge."

"Mean son-of-a-bitch. Wa'al, I'll keep an eye out for him. Looks like Kelleray an' them other two figured to kill Juanito. Shut him up for good."

At Aleman's Barn Miguel was overjoyed at the way things had turned out, Juanito cleared of the murder charge.

After much free whiskey, the sheriff got Lassiter aside. "Long as Kelleray's dead, let's leave Margaret Ryerson's name out of this. We'll say Kelleray killed Toby Miles because of the money he owed him, an' then framed Juanito for it."

Lassiter smiled to himself. Lambert didn't want to experience Charlie Ryerson's wrath. "All right with me. You convince the others."

An hour later the sheriff and his men departed, the two dead men lashed to the horses Lassiter had appropriated the night of the jailbreak. The third horse that had turned up lame was at a mountain ranch. Lambert would have a long ride to reclaim that one. Lassiter had no intention of doing it.

He found Elnora in the store, using a feather duster. It seemed to Lassiter that it was the first time the place had been touched in weeks. Elnora saw him.

"We'll start living again," she said to Lassiter. He leaned tiredly against a counter, watching the handsome face. No sound in the big room with its shelves depleted of stock, only the whisper of the duster. They were alone in that part of the building.

"I want to thank you for what you did for Juanito," she said. She walked toward him, the duster over her shoulder carried like a rifle. She halted, looking up into his face. "Maybe I wish I could express my thanks in a way that would please us both. But when I make a bargain I keep it. I made one when I married Miguel."

Lassiter wondered about that bargain. What if he made a move? There was no one else around. Juanito was upstairs, asleep, exhausted after his ordeal. Miguel was in the other end of the building at the saloon, waiting on some customers. He was cheerful and apparently much improved in health.

Elnora's lips relaxed. "Lassiter, don't look so serious. I want to be your friend." She offered her hand, which he took. The fingers were soft, warm. He was wondering just how solid that bargain she had made might be after another year or so. He hoped Miguel never had to find out.

That evening Miguel insisted on a farewell dinner before Lassiter headed north again. Elnora cooked a roast of beef. Juanito seemed glum instead of elated at being cleared of the murder charge.

Miguel noted Juanito's mood. "It's that Ryerson girl,"

he whispered, leaning toward the lamp at Lassiter's end of the table. "She is not for him, never was. He'll get over it. Juanito is young. Plenty of girls for him."

Miguel had had too much wine at the victory dinner and his voice carried. Juanito looked across the table. "You don't have to worry about Margaret Ryerson. She's one female I *don't* want to see."

Miguel seemed embarrassed that his remarks had been overheard. "Do not hate her, Juanito, and you sound as if you do."

Juanito took a sip from his wine glass and stared at shadows cast by lamplight on the dining room wall.

"It's wrong to hate anyone," Elnora put in, faintly worried when Juanito failed to respond.

Before leaving in the morning, Lassiter had a few words with Juanito. "Treat Miguel just as you always have. As your father. It'll please the old man and it costs you nothing."

"I . . . I'll try."

"*Do* it!"

Juanito gave him a twisted smile. "Running my life again, blood brother?"

Miguel appeared at the corral where Lassiter was saddling up. Miguel was loaning him a mount until he could pick up his own at the county seat.

"You are truly Juanito's blood brother and you saved his life," Miguel said gravely in Spanish. "That oath you took, my friend, has great power. I think you understand that now."

Lassiter only shrugged. He didn't believe in such nonsense. He intended that the blood brother business was finished. He'd had enough. It didn't turn out that way, however.

Chapter Thirteen

A few days later, Lassiter picked up his rifle at the Banner County Jail. It had been turned over to Lambert when Lassiter left the weapon in his hotel room.

"Got one thing to say," the sheriff grunted, looking up at him from his desk. "You saved Juanito's hide an' I don't begrudge you that. But he's got wild blood in him from somewheres. If he really goes bad, then I'll figure you're as much to blame as him. For not stayin' here to keep an eye on him."

"Blood brother is one thing. Nursemaid something else."

"I seen how Juanito was in his usual surly mood even after he was cleared."

"He's been through hell."

"So's a lot of other folks." Lambert eyed him. "I heard that them cow thievin' Monagals was seen recent over at Prescott. Mebby so. Mebby not. I'm remembering what Kelleray said about you an' them."

"He was lying."

"Just don't give me no more trouble, Lassiter."

"I don't figure to."

Lambert scribbled a release order which he thrust at Lassiter.

"This'll git you your hoss." The sheriff cocked an eye at him. "'Spose you know, there'll be a sizeable feed bill."

"County should pay. I had to leave town on rather short notice."

Lambert reddened, remembering the short notice, him paraded along the street with twin muzzles of a shotgun poking him in the back.

"One time you ain't gonna git your own way, Lassiter. By god, you badgered an' bedeviled me long enough. You pay that feed bill or I'll come after you with a warrant for defrauding Sam Englemann outa his bill."

"Don't get so riled. I'll pay the bill."

"Tell you the truth, Lassiter, I hope you *never* come back to Banner County."

Lassiter smiled to himself. For some years, sheriffs had been expressing the hope that he would stay out of their territory.

At the livery barn a curious crowd gathered. Only a few days ago they would have shot him on sight, but now they seemed to regard him as a hero for saving Juanito Aleman whom they had been so eager to hang. Down the block, in the shadow of the jail and two tall trees, the gallows was a skeletal reminder of the impermanence of life on the frontier. Lassiter booted his rifle, strapped on a bedroll and led his horse out through a rear door, away from the onlookers.

He was surprised to see Margaret Ryerson at the county seat, broodingly beautiful. She came up to him and put out her hand. Lassiter took it, wondering at his change of luck. The second attractive female in recent days who had offered her hand. It seemed he was destined to go no farther with either of them.

"When you talked to Juanito did he mention me?" she asked bluntly, withdrawing her hand from his.

Lassiter decided that responsibility for reestablishing a romance was not the function of a blood brother. Let Juanito ride his own horse. Then he thought, what the hell, just this once.

"Why don't you ride down and see him?" he suggested.

"It's his place to see me." Then her lip curled. "Besides, my father would never allow me to ride down there now. After what's happened." She ground her teeth in frustration; they were large, very white against the faint tan of her face. Her cheekbones were high, the brows arched, brown eyes brooding again.

"Seems like your father's got you in harness."

"In harness, yes I admit it. I thought Juanito had the backbone to defy my father and come to see me. Well, I guess he doesn't. So that's the end of it."

"Why does he need backbone to come and see a girl?"

"It's a special case. His father and mine dislike each other for reasons I can't imagine. Juanito is as much in harness to his own father as I am to mine."

He wondered how long it would be before she heard the story of Miguel's confession; that he wasn't Juanito's father. He watched her eyes, saw the steel in them. A man needed that in a wife for this rough country. Also there was a touch of devilment, which could make the nights a joy.

"If I had good sense," she said, a taut smile on the red lips, "I'd run off with the notorious Lassiter. It would serve my father right."

"You speak right out, I'll say that."

"Usually I'm not so outspoken."

"I bring it out in you, huh?" His eyes danced.

"Perhaps I feel we're kindred souls." She laughed, more of a choking sound of grief than any display of pleasure. No doubt her thoughts were on Juanito. He was no fool, she certainly wasn't dwelling on Lassiter, no matter what she had just suggested. But in the next breath she surprised him.

"I always ride out east road in the mornings. The only road bordered with poplars on the ranch. You can't miss it. I always ride alone. I'll be home tomorrow." She stood with head back, dark hair shining in the sunlight, looking defiantly up into his face. He did not miss the challenge in her eyes.

He told himself it was all over between this spirited young female and Juanito Aleman. Juanito was a fool to be so stiff-necked.

"The east road, lined with poplars," he murmured. "What time in the morning?"

"Not tomorrow, the day after. But I'll be up then at sunup. That's when I always ride."

"You get up with the birds, eh?"

"If I think the day holds a promise of something interesting."

Wagons rumbled in the street. Down the block, some men were arguing about the new railroad that would reach Brightwater in another year.

"I also like days that hold promise," he told her with a faint grin.

She gave him a nod and then wheeled and walked rapidly away, her fine figure only partially subdued by blouse and divided riding skirt. Garments intended to dampen prurient thoughts.

Well, in all this blood brother business he had earned a bonus, for sure. In the space of only a few weeks he had settled the Monagal feud in the only way possible, in violent death. And at the risk of his own life. Then there had been the three men who had jumped him out of Denver. Not to mention the hazardous night he had abducted a sheriff. And after those narrow escapes there had been the recent business with Kelleray and his two friends. It suddenly reminded him of the one who had fled. What had Kelleray called him? Sawbridge.

Short hairs twitched at the back of his neck. Just because a man had ducked out of a gunfight did not necessarily mean he was a coward. Maybe one of those who believed there was a time to fight and a time to run.

How careless to have stood on the walk, hat in hand, talking with the Ryerson girl, his back not against a building front as was his habit, but to the street. Kelleray's missing friend could easily have shot him down, if he wanted to avenge the deaths of Kelleray and the other one Lassiter had killed.

And come to think of it, what was Maggie Ryerson's motive in suggesting a rendezvous? A trap?

Was she the kind of sultry female who possibly sought revenge against males of the world in strange ways? Juanito had rejected her, no denying that. Maybe the XR crew breaking a few of his bones would soothe her troubled soul.

Hell with her. He had other things to do.

He was thinking of Bessie as he rode north. A mile out of town he heard hoofbeats. Looking around, he saw Margaret Ryerson riding toward him. She was mounted on a big red stallion that seemed too much horse for the average female to handle. But he had already decided she was not average.

"So you were going to leave town and ignore me," she accused.

"Looks like it."

She reined in, her cool appraisal irritating him. She said, "You had no intention of meeting me on the ranch road."

"Not on XR ranch road. *Your* road. I'm no fool."

"I wanted us to have a talk . . . is all."

"So it's only talk you wanted," he said with a twist of his lips.

"Did you possibly think there was more to it than that?"

"Go play your games with somebody else, Miss Ryerson." He started away.

"Wait!" A small pearl-handled lady's revolver appeared from a pocket of her riding skirt. "I fire three shots in the air and there'll be a swarm of men riding out of town in answer to my distress signal."

"If you want to see people get hurt, why go ahead. Shoot." He rode away at a walk.

She caught up with him. He gave her a sidelong glance, noticing that she nervously bit that full and fetching underlip.

"What I really want is to hire you for a job," she blurted.

"You had your chance in town to hire me. You and your bold talk about ranch roads. Quite an actress, aren't you?" Their eyes locked and finally she was the one to lower hers.

"Lassiter, I do want to hire you. I know what's changed Juanito. His stepmother . . ."

"People change themselves. Others don't change them."

"Please spare me philosophy." Then the steel went out of her eyes. "Help me, Lassiter."

"Help you? Why?" They were moving slowly along the road side by side.

"Because I need you. The things you've done. I heard about them and I'm impressed."

For a moment he felt like laughing. Then he looked around at her. The warm afternoon had put a sheen of moisture on her high forehead. He caught a scent of lavender as she moved her horse close so that their legs touched. Two top buttons of her beige blouse had somehow come unfastened. When she shifted her body in the saddle he could see the lacy top edge of a camisole.

"Just what do you think I can do about Senora Aleman?" he asked, one eye on her gun.

"She's disruptive. Juanito's in love with her. I'm sure of it."

Margaret gestured hopelessly with her right hand that still held the revolver. It was practically under his nose. He didn't lose the opportunity to twist it out of her grasp. She did not resist.

"Makes me nervous, somebody waving a gun in my face," he told her gruffly.

"It was only to show you that I mean business."

"Business?"

"Miguel Aleman's young wife."

"As I said before, what do you think I can do?"

"Use your charm. Get her to run away with you."

"And that'll bring Juanito back to you?"

She seemed suddenly uncertain. "I . . . I think so."

Lassiter shook his head. "Be practical. He was in love with you once, but he's changed. There's no way in the world you can get him back. Unless he wants to come back."

"The worldly-wise Lassiter," she said sarcastically.

"Once people fall out of love, it's over."

Her shoulders stiffened and she said in surprise, "Juanito *told* you he no longer loves me?"

Lassiter thought back to Juanito's response when Margaret Ryerson's name had come up. It had been an expression of pure hatred, rather than just a falling out of love.

"He did tell you, didn't he?" she persisted, studying

his face. Then her lips paled. "You don't have to admit it. Your silence is enough for me."

"You've got to remember it's a bad time for him. He came within a few hours of having his neck snapped on a gallows . . ."

"And you're the one who saved him. I heard how you came out of the jail with Sheriff Lambert and Juanito. Everyone says you were so incredibly calm about it all . . ."

"Sometimes fear doesn't show through."

"Nonsense. I'm sure there wasn't a shred of fear in you that night."

"You better head for home. I've got a long ride ahead of me."

"I'm going with you. Until you promise to work for me. And get Elnora Aleman out of Banner County."

"That's childish."

"I am no child, Mr. Lassiter."

He looked her over. "Woman on the outside, maybe. But under the skin you're twelve years old."

That stung her. "For your information, I was sent away to school in California. I soon learned that young ladies have considerably more freedom there than they do here. *I am no child.*"

"Do tell."

"I have sampled enough of life to know what I'm talking about."

His hoot of laughter tightened her eyes.

"Give me back my gun." She thrust out a hand for it, the fingers long and slim, the nails polished. Then, under his hard gaze, she withdrew her hand.

"You're a kid trying to play grown-up games," he said coldly. "Get back to town." He jerked a thumb southward.

"I happen to know that men with considerable

charm, such as yourself, can make a woman do . . . do most anything." Her face flushed under its light tan. "You could persuade Elnora Aleman to run away with you."

"You must sit up all hours of the night reading dime novels."

"I'll pay you one thousand dollars if you get rid of Juanito's stepmother."

"Deprive Miguel of his wife?" Lassiter shook his head.

"She's no wife to him."

"Now you're suddenly an authority on bedrooms."

"No need to get quite so earthy, Lassiter."

"You're the one opened up this can of worms. I'm riding on. If you try to keep up with me you'll wear out your horse and be afoot."

He sank in the spurs and his horse leaped ahead. But she was right behind him. "You've got my gun!"

He reined in, their horses nearly colliding. Angrily he jacked the shells out of her revolver and threw them into a deep canyon to the left of the road. Then he thrust the revolver into her hand.

"I don't have more shells with me," she protested. "If you abandon me and I get into trouble because I can't defend myself . . ."

"Maybe you're hard of hearing, Miss Ryerson. I'm riding on . . . alone!"

Again he spurred away. He didn't look around. But after a few miles he halted on a rise of ground. She was stubbornly riding across the flats below. Her hair had come uncoiled and spilled across her shoulders.

He swore under his breath, considered pushing on and to hell with her. But it was rough country and she was a girl alone. And if he did abandon her and something happened . . . Well, wouldn't hurt to have another talk with her, he told himself wryly. His horse had smelled water and was whinnying. He let it have its head, moving off into scrubby pines for a quarter of a mile, leaving deep tracks in the loose soil, until he could see a small lake reflecting sunlight through the branches of taller trees.

He was sitting on a rock in the late afternoon, smoking a thin Mexican cigar Miguel had given him when she finally rode up. Her horse was streaked with sweat in the climb from the flats, foam at the muzzle.

"You don't think much of horse flesh," he accused.

"Lassiter, you set a fast pace. But I vowed to keep up with you." She slid to the ground.

"Your father will have half the county out looking for you."

"He thinks I'm spending the night in Brightwater with the Richards. Their daughter Jennifer is supposed to be a good influence." She gave a bark of laughter.

"Staying the night," Lassiter mused as he studied her through a faint haze of cigar smoke.

"That water looks inviting," she said, pointing at the small lake. "I feel as if I'm coated with an inch of dust."

"Enjoy your bath. I'll be heading out."

She looked exasperated. "I am presenting a challenge. Don't you know one when you see it?"

"Go challenge the lake."

She started to speak; her voice trembled. Standing in the slanting shadows of tall trees she seemed suddenly vulnerable, not at all sure of herself. It was a time to move in, but he fought it. There was absolutely no sense in getting entangled with her, shouted his better judgment. He was already enmeshed in the Aleman family affairs and this girl was certainly an offshoot of that problem. Juanito's problem, should he ever again decide to pursue the romance. Which was highly unlikely. The cold sullenness that Lassiter had disliked in the younger man for so long had returned when Margaret Ryerson's name came up.

And now this girl, used to having her own way with everyone but her father was trying to tempt him into accepting the job of getting Elnora Aleman out of her life. Even if he took the bait, he felt that at the last minute she'd lose her nerve. He didn't believe her hints of promiscuity out in California.

She stood now with her blouse unbuttoned, hanging loose. He could see her breasts, rather small but shapely, half-hidden by the folds of silk and the camisole.

"Button your shirt," he said gruffly. "I'm riding you back to town."

"Lassiter, you're a coward."

"Am I?"

"Afraid to . . . to take . . ." Boldness collapsed as her voice weakened. She tried to cover it with a shaky smile.

He swung into the saddle, turned his horse. He could see that she had pushed down the camisole, her upper body nearly bared. Sunlight through overhead branches touched the breasts with their roseate nipples.

When he started to rein his horse toward the road, she yelled at him. "Damn you, Lassiter, you're making a *fool* of me!"

"You're making it of yourself. Get your clothes on. You're coming back to town if I have to tie you to the saddle . . ."

He turned his head, intending to look back at her. And in that bare second he saw the figure in the brush, saw the gun. It exploded almost in his face.

This followed by a man's wild shout. Lassiter's horse shied. Instinctively and foolishly in trying to duck a bullet, Lassiter rolled off the rump of the animal and crashed to the ground. A great halo of light burst behind his eyeballs. The last thing he heard was Maggie Ryerson's scream of terror.

Chapter Fourteen

This, then, was death. The thought ripped at him from a deepening darkness of his mind. As he lay inert, the scream was repeated. Then a male stream of obscenities.

"You an' your goddamn fingernails!" This followed by a flat meaty sound; an open hand striking flesh.

Lassiter's eyelids flew open. Somehow he pulled himself to a sitting position, his head filled with a clang of bells. He was vaguely aware of warm blood on his neck.

Instinctively, he reached for his gun; fingertips brushed an empty holster. In a haze he saw the weapon lying in gravel a few feet away. He also saw the rock, half-buried in the ground, where he obviously struck the back of his head when he fell. His gaze swept in the direction of the lake and Maggie Ryerson's continuing screams, muffled now. A man's hand, large enough to cover the lower half of his face, had been clamped over nose and mouth. The other hand was ripping at what remained of her clothing.

Desperately Lassiter tried to adjust his vision; everything was in triplicate. His arms felt as if weighted with chains.

He could see her assailant's broad back, the powerful shoulders. The man's hat had been knocked off. Shaggy hair hung over the collar of a black shirt. He had holstered his gun, an ivory-butted weapon that jiggled in his battle with the slender girl. Then he was turned so that Lassiter could see deep scratches on a cheek, the rivulets spilling blood. She tried to claw him again. He caught both of her wrists in his one hand.

No matter what Lassiter might have thought of her as a conniving young female, he had to admit that she was a fighter. She jacknifed her body and kicked herself away from him. But as she tried to run, he lunged, one long arm knocking her legs out from under her. She fell. When she rolled over on her back, trying to get away, he fell on her. His weight pinned her to the ground.

"So goddamn high an' mighty all the time I was at XR. Well, Chick's dead, so they tell me. He always figured you as his little prize. Well, I got the prize now . . ."

In Lassiter's clearing head came recognition. He remembered the man. Sawbridge. One of those with Chick Kelleray, the one who had fled. Even in town Lassiter had sensed that someone might be stalking him. He should have listened to his hunches. How well he knew it now; the girl writhing on the ground and Sawbridge trying to anchor those lively legs so he could achieve the purpose of his assault.

There was one trouble with the scene from Lassiter's viewpoint. He was no longer seeing everything in triplicate, now they were merely double, the images fairly well spaced so that he could not really pinpoint the difference between which were real and which the result of distorted vision.

He started to get up. But the ground seemed to move and tilted at such an angle that he had the feeling he was about to slide off the earth. He lost his balance, fell back on the seat of his pants.

Maggie Ryerson saw him then, her stricken features appearing above Sawbridge's shoulder. *"Lassiter!"*

Sawbridge had his face buried in the girl's chest. He jerked upright at the threat of danger from a man he had considered out of it. He pawed for his gun, sprang up. Lassiter rolled over and over, the clangorous darkness of his mind seeming to clear in a flash. One bullet fanned a sheaf of pine needles against the side of his face as it plowed the ground where he had been but an instant before. Lassiter's hand closed over his dropped gun. He snapped off a shot, aiming with pure instinct. Sawbridge's second bullet whacked a tree limb, for his aim was off, the one from Lassiter's gun having already slammed into him. Sawbridge was flung backward, arms lifted overhead as if in worship of the splintered sunlight beaming through the trees. His mouth sagged and emptied itself of his own blood. He collapsed, life fading from his eyes before he struck the ground.

Maggie Ryerson sprang up, holding what was left of tattered clothing about her as she stared down at the figure on the ground. She shuddered, then sprinted toward Lassiter. Her silk shirt dangled by one sleeve, the divided riding skirt that had been ripped by powerful fingers flopped in strips against her scissoring legs in flight.

"Lassiter, Lassiter, I thought you were dead . . . I thought he'd killed you."

She clung to him, gasping for breath. Then her lips darted hungrily, almost desperately about his face. One of her cheeks was reddened, slightly swollen where the assailant had struck her.

"I wanted the son-of-a-bitch to hang," Lassiter panted.

"Oh, god no! I would have had to testify and it would have been awful. Believe me, in the eyes of Banner County I'd have been as guilty as he."

"Then Banner County doesn't have very damn much to be proud of."

She buried her face in his shoulder. "That man . . . he *is* dead, isn't he?"

"There's not much left of the back of his head. Let's get out of here. We'll leave the bastard for the buzzards."

Because of the condition of her clothing, he undid his bedroll and gave her a blanket. It would help cover her body. They rode through the trees, following a creek that was fed by the small mountain lake.

For the first time she noticed his wound and seemed shocked. "Lassiter, there's a gash on the back of your head."

"I took a good whack when I hit the ground."

"It hurts terribly, I imagine."

"I've had worse."

She hunched her shoulders, pulling the blanket tighter about her upper body. "God, I was frightened. I never thought it could come so close . . . rape. What an ugly word."

"Killing's too good for his kind."

"Thank goodness I don't have to see him stand trial. It would be almost as bad as the horror itself. That's why it's rare for a woman to swear out a complaint. The stigma, not so much on the rapist, but on the woman. For letting it happen."

"He was after me, not you."

"You?" She turned in the saddle to stare. He told her about the gunfight, how Sawbridge had fled after his friend had been killed.

"Sight of you in that unbuttoned shirt was too much for him," Lassiter said thinly. "Too much for me, really. I got careless and he got a bead on me."

"I . . . I distracted you . . ."

"For a second there I thought it was going to be my last view of a lush female body." He gave her a twisted smile.

"I'm sorry, Lassiter."

"Something you'd better cut out."

"What?"

"Teasing a man. You could wind up dead."

"When you . . . you refused to have anything to do with me . . ." She licked her lips. "It was something I simply couldn't understand. It stung my pride." She reached out through a fold of the blanket and gripped his arm. "Do you suppose I'm in love with you, Lassiter?"

"No." But he couldn't deny the softness of her voice when she said it.

"I've been impressed ever since I heard how you defied the whole town in order to free Juanito."

"Make your peace with him," he said roughly, not liking it that he could feel himself melting. What he didn't want was the burden of an adolescent female. And yet . . . He looked at her half-clothed figure in the blanket, riding proudly with head back. In the sparse light in the shadowed trees she had the dignity of an Indian princess.

Her voice was wistful for a moment. "I've only loved two men . . . Juanito and . . ." She didn't finish it. "But Juanito is the one that hurts. The other was when I was in California. And now Juanito hates me."

"If he does, he'll get over it."

Late afternoon birdsong drifted from the thickets. The sun glowed like an orange ball on the horizon.

Maggie Ryerson said, "Three times I've been in love in my short lifetime."

"You said two . . . Juanito and somebody else."

"The third one is you."

He thought about it for a moment, his eyes sweeping ahead to a clearing, looking for reasonably level ground for a camp site. He found it.

There was arnica in his warbag which she used on the gash at the back of his head. Her fingers were gentle. "That was an awful blow," she said, sitting back on her heels, holding the blanket about her with one hand.

"I'll fix us some supper," he muttered.

"You're taking me with you after all," she said happily, but he killed that hope with a shake of the head.

"You can't go back to town looking like that. I'll get you something to wear when the store opens in the morning."

Her eyes danced. "By morning you may change your mind."

He got up, his head throbbing, and hunted for firewood. He returned with an armload.

"I can cook," she said, "a little. But I'm willing to learn." Her sidelong glance was lively. "You can teach me ever so much, Lassiter."

They ate bacon and biscuits in the starry early evening, drank her coffee which he said was strong enough to kill a rattlesnake. They shared his one plate and cup.

"I do love you, Lassiter . . ."

"You're too young to know what it means."

"I want to go with you. No matter where."

"To get even with your father."

"I've put that out of my mind."

"You'd soon get damned sick of my kind of life, young lady."

"Maggie is the name," she reminded.

She moved her head slightly so that her eyes seemed

to catch the starlight. Her lips were close, too close to ignore. What the hell. And besides, she wore one of his blankets. If the night turned chilly here in the high country, which it probably would, they'd need it in the bedroll before morning.

She was right about one thing. Somewhere in her young life, whether at school in California or perhaps with Juanito, she had already sampled the joys. Lassiter could only speculate on who it might have been. Not that it mattered. Virginity had never appealed to him. Frankly, he was relieved in not having to cope with it.

In the morning they made love again, just as the sun was beginning to outshine the remaining stars. He found that enjoying her could easily become a habit it might be hard to break. He decided, however, to keep such knowledge to himself. At breakfast he became gruff, hoping his mood would discourage her. She seemed pleased, almost as if sensing he covered his own feelings in such a manner.

His pressing problem was to get her home and in new clothes to cover her near-nakedness. All the way down the mountain he had to keep eyes peeled in both directions on the road. It wouldn't do for anyone to see the heiress of XR ranch attired in a blanket that barely reached gleaming thighs to be seen through a tattered skirt.

Instead of pushing on to Brightwater, the county seat, he swung east, taking a short cut to Kendall Springs. He left her in a clump of cottonwoods on the outskirts of town. At the store he discussed his problem with a thin-faced clerk. He wanted shirt and Levis, "For a kid at the ranch. Comes up to my shoulder. And . . . well, you better make the pants a little big in the seat . . ."

"For a girl?" the clerk asked, brows lifted.

Lassiter pretended to be examining a Remington in a showcase.

It was nearly noon, Maggie attired in the stiff new clothing, that they reached the XR ranch road. She had kept the torn skirt and shirt wadded in the same gunny-sack that had contained the new clothes bought for her at Kendall Springs.

"To keep as a reminder that I must never let myself get in that position again," she had told him.

He didn't argue. If she wanted to keep a handful of rags, it was her business.

By then she was convinced that he intended to go it alone; he wanted no encumbrance of a female, no matter how fetching she might be. At first Maggie sulked, then she brightened. But when they reached the ranch road her mood darkened.

There was the problem of her father's wrath should he learn she hadn't stayed with friends in town as she had intended. She would say that the Hammond woman had been taken ill.

"I'll make up a story about being restless," Maggie said, "and say I followed a freight outfit all the way to the ranch road. He raises hell if he thinks I ride anywhere alone. Cussing like that doesn't make me sound like much of a lady, now does it?"

"In my blankets you weren't much of a lady."

"Thank God you noticed."

There was always the possibility she could slip into the big house without being seen, no matter the hour. She lived in one wing, he in another. They rarely saw each other except at an occasional evening meal.

When they finally parted, Lassiter put out his hand. She looked at the brown fingers, the sinewy wrist, then up into his eyes. "Is that all I get . . . after last night?"

"Look, try and make it up with Juanito," he said seriously.

"I can't melt a wall of ice."

"You can if you try. He needs you. And you sure as hell need him." She did need a man, that much he had learned in the wild night on the mountain. And that man might as well be Juanito, he told himself. In spite of his claim that a dead love could never be revived, he hoped that in this case he was wrong. She and Juanito had been in love once, he pointed out. They could be again, with a little effort from the two of them. He sensed she was still deeply attached to Juanito. Because of Juanito's aloofness since being cleared of the murder charge, her pride had prevented her from showing it. If Juanito could ever unfreeze his emotions.

For sure, Juanito must have been thawed out at least once with her. Or *somebody* had.

She finally shook his hand, her fingers lingering. "Lassiter, I'll never forget you."

"Take your new clothes and go home." He flashed her a grin and tilted his head in the direction of the big house in the distance that was nearly hidden by cottonwoods.

Maggie looked down at the baggy shirt and Levis. "I'll have to sneak into the house," she laughed. Then she added, soberly, "I'll send you money for the clothes. Just tell me where."

He didn't want to give an address. She just might show up and if she did, it might please him too much. Last night had been too good; a man could easily get into the habit of wanting and needing on a regular basis the luxury of such an outstanding human being as Margaret Ryerson.

And it was tempting in the cool poplars and the natural hiding places in thick brush, to make the farewell something they would both remember. But the risk was too great. Even though he sensed she was ready to accept the gamble that no one would come along the ranch road.

"I'm hoping you and Juanito have lots of kids. Name one of them after me."

"And just what is your name?"

"Lassiter."

"Only Lassiter? Nothing else?"

"That's it. On the other hand, it wouldn't be such a good idea to saddle a kid with my name." He gave her a nod of his head. "Remember what I said about Juanito. Write him a letter, at least."

"I wrote him and wrote him when he was in jail. He never replied . . . not once.."

"And he wrote you."

She looked at him. "He told you?"

"Yeah."

Her face brightened. "My father . . ."

"A man of influence, for sure."

She seemed close to tears as she rode away without looking back.

As she neared the house, she wondered if it was asking for trouble to keep the torn clothing that was to remind her of a close call. The snooping housekeeper might find the garments.

Removing the gunnysack from her saddlebag, she tossed it and its contents into thick brush and rode on.

Hal Dempster, the sixth foreman in two years at XR, was riding in from a horse pen when he happened to see Margaret Ryerson through the screen of poplars toss a sack into the brush.

Being of a curious nature, he wondered just what the hell she had thrown away . . .

Chapter Fifteen

Lassiter cut west and north, away from the XR road. He was still on XR property some miles later when he heard a drumming of hoofs. He loosened his Winchester in the boot and looked over his shoulder. Some dozen riders were sweeping toward him from a fold of sere hills. He recognized the beefy, arrogant figure of Charlie Ryerson in the lead.

Disaster spun across his mind. *The vindictive bitch had confessed all to her father . . .*

Knowing it was useless to try and outrun a superior force on a weary horse, he reined in. They might shoot him, but he'd make damn sure that Ryerson reached hell's front door at the same time.

He was a little surprised when Ryerson waved his men aside and came on alone.

"Want words with you, Lassiter."

Lassiter gave him a sour smile. "You bring half your crew along just to have words?"

"Just what the hell are you doing on my property?"

"Took a shortcut," Lassiter said.

"On my way north to fetch my daughter and I find you here." Ryerson's small eyes probed. "Here's what I want to say. I've been forced to accept Sheriff Lambert's story that he witnessed Chick Kelleray's confession."

Elnora Aleman had been the witness that counted, Lassiter wanted to say. Otherwise . . .

"Never did like that son-of-a-bitch, Kelleray," Ryerson grumbled. "Though he did work at XR for a spell."

"Surprised you'd hire such a cutthroat."

"I like to hire tough men. Then if they go over the edge, I kick them out. Nothing like a feeling of power to keep the sap rising in a man." Ryerson's smile was arrogant, all teeth.

"I pity this territory if you're appointed governor."

"And when I am appointed, make sure you never displease me in any way."

Lassiter shrugged. The XR men had dismounted twenty yards across the flats, to stand by their horses, smoking, eyes watchful for any signal from Ryerson. Should Ryerson be that foolish, this could turn out to be the best day of Maggie Ryerson's life. She would be rid of a domineering father. That she'd also be rid of last night's lover, also crossed Lassiter's mind. At least Maggie apparently had been able to slip into the big house without being seen. What Ryerson's reaction would be when he learned she hadn't spent the night at Brightwater as planned, would be another matter.

"Juanito made threats when he's been drunk," Ryerson said. "I don't like it worth a damn that he singles me out as some kind of ogre."

"His parents were killed when he was a baby. He's bitter."

Ryerson met his eyes. "You think I had a hand in it. Don't know where that damn story got started. But it's a lie."

"Why did your men beat up Miguel? Send him home in a wagon?"

"Because Miguel came over here wearing a gun. I won't stand for that, even though I've considered him a friend of long standing." Ryerson rubbed his jaw. "I could have ordered him arrested. Possibly my men did get too rough, but maybe it'll teach Miguel a lesson."

"Seal his lips, you mean."

"Listen to me, Lassiter. Miguel may not be so old in years, but he is in mind. He's become demented, mainly because of his young wife. Obviously she's too much for him."

"Miguel never complained that she's too much for him."

Ryerson ignored the sarcasm. "Miguel's been making up these stories about what might have happened years ago. I've been most tolerant of Miguel, even though he's Mexican . . ."

"They were here two hundred years before the Anglos."

"I don't need a history lesson. Those cutthroat Mexicans you seem to defend, have been driven out . . . a lot of them at any rate. And Miguel repays my tolerance by spreading lies."

Lassiter neck reined his horse to get the sun out of his eyes. He was angry enough to do something foolish, even against the odds. He was on XR property. And bunched not far away from a dozen XR riders.

"You think only Miguel is left to remember the day you found two suspected horse thieves?"

"Careful, Lassiter . . ."

"Without even giving them a chance to explain, you and the others gunned them down."

"If Miguel told you that, he lies!"

"One of your friends of that day is dead. The other is ranching in Oregon. Maybe I know his name. Maybe in a few weeks I'll ride up there and ask him to his face if Miguel lies."

Ryerson swallowed. "You think any man would be

fool enough to admit a thing like that . . . even if it were true?"

Out on the flats the XR men were getting restless. Some of them had remounted, sitting stiffly in the saddle. Ryerson's booming anger had carried that far and they were ready for trouble. Lassiter had heard stories about the XR crew and their possible lack of loyalty in a crisis, to the despot who paid their wages. But this was no time to test it. Lassiter put a brake on his temper. Ryerson crowded his horse closer to Lassiter's mount, the eyes bright with suppressed rage. "Tell you something, Lassiter. I don't give a damn how Sheriff Lambert feels, but I think you should stand trial for assaulting a law officer. And stealing horses."

"Lambert isn't pressing charges."

"Tod is getting soft in the head." Ryerson's round face, with its tracery of veins at the cheeks, seemed to swell. "We need a new sheriff, young and aggressive. If we'd had him the other night, you'd never have gotten away with that jailbreak."

"Better to hang an innocent man?" Lassiter couldn't help flinging at him.

"Maybe I'm not so sure he's innocent. You're a clever bastard, Lassiter, with cool nerve. For all I know, maybe you forced Chick Kelleray to confess to something he didn't do."

"That's absurd and you know it."

"One thing to remember and this is mainly what I wanted to say to you today, Lassiter," Ryerson leveled a meaty forefinger. "If Juanito Aleman should go berserk again, you're the one I'll hold responsible." It was a dismissal. Ryerson turned his horse.

"I'll remember," Lassiter muttered angrily.

He rode away, cold sweat dampening the back of his shirt. He had pushed Ryerson to the edge.

He had already told Miguel he was going back to El Paso, because by now the anger against him would have subsided. And if it hadn't? Well, sometimes it was best to face up to a thing, get it over with. El Paso was one of his favorite cities and he had no intention of abandoning its pleasures and opportunities just because a gambling house had been displeased when he trimmed a mining engineer at high-stakes poker who they'd intended to fleece.

In El Paso he found that some of his friends had moved on as well as a few of his enemies. It was relatively quiet across the border for a change. From time to time his thoughts returned to Charlie Ryerson, who had practically ordered him out of Banner County. His thoughts returning more pleasantly to the daughter and their wild night in the mountains.

He renewed acquaintances with several females.

But he began to itch for some real action . . .

At Aleman's Barn Elnora studied the rather handsome Jud Pryor who had located their horses. How fortunate they were, for rustlers had been working in the area. Pryor was probably in his early thirties. In some ways he reminded her of Lassiter, who had left them weeks ago. This Jud Pryor might be the answer to her prayers. When she discussed it with Miguel, he told her to make the decision. He seemed to have lost interest in the operation of Aleman's Barn.

She asked the soft-spoken Pryor if he wanted a job.

"Ma'am, it'd be a real pleasure to work for *you*."

She found herself blushing, but met his eyes. "You'll be working for my husband," she said so he wouldn't misunderstand.

When Juanito returned home after a three day absence, Elnora hoped to use Pryor as an incentive to get him to pitch in and do his share around the place.

But Juanito's only response was to say gravely, "Elnora, it will soon be over. I'll fix things . . . for both of us."

It made her feel uneasy. She tried to get him to explain, but his only reaction was a familiar tight smile which she tried to interpret as bitter or perhaps faintly triumphant. That Pryor had been hired to take over duties that should be Juanito's seemed not to concern the younger man in the least. Elnora was baffled, worried.

During the night she thought of what Juanito had said: "It'll soon be over. I'll fix things . . . for both of us."

What in the world had he meant?

In the morning she asked him again to explain. He only shrugged and smiled. Then she voiced a growing suspicion; little things that Juanito had let slip.

"Have you been seeing Maggie Ryerson again?" thinking it might pry open those reluctant lips.

Mention of Maggie brought a strange look to his light gray eyes that made her wonder if possibly the ordeal of being so near to execution had in some way affected his mind. It was not the first time she had wondered about it.

Jud Pryor had been on the job three weeks when a couple that had been working for them, suddenly quit. They were the Hartleys, Tom and Dora. Tom had worked in the bar before Jud Pryor was hired, but was easily intimidated by some of the drunken cowhands. Pryor handled trouble with ease. Tom seemed to enjoy his new role as handyman. Dora did the cooking, which relieved Elnora of that time-consuming task.

One morning Elnora came downstairs to find that Dora Hartley had not put on a pot of fresh coffee as usual. Nor was she about to. She and her husband had just finished loading their few possessions into a spring wagon and were ready to pull out.

Elnora ran to the yard, skirts hiked high to keep from tripping. But she was too late. They were already on the road.

She called to them, but neither of the Hartleys looked around. Tom was using a whip on his team, sending them into a frenzied run. She had a strange feeling that something or someone had frightened them away.

Pryor came to stand at Elnora's side. "We'll get along without them," he said.

"What made them leave so abruptly?"

"Husband and wife argument, near as I could make out."

"Seems that we'll have to rely on you, Jud."

He looked down into her face out of bright hazel eyes. Lately he reminded her of someone she had seen before. But who?

He said, "First time you've called me Jud." He smiled.

That was it, the smile. Where had she seen such a smile before? She decided not to make anything out of the fact that she had used his first name. And he was waiting for her comment.

She had to admit that Pryor in his soft-spoken manner kept trouble in the saloon to a minimum.

Juanito, when he came home, seemed uninterested that the Hartleys had suddenly quit.

"This time go up to the county seat and hire somebody who'll be reliable," Juanito suggested. "Don't pick on drifters. They're bad luck."

"I was a drifter before I married your . . ." She still

found it hard not to refer to Miguel as his father. "Before I married Miguel."

"I know." His smile was warm for a change. "You were one of the good drifters."

That pleased her. "Why don't you do the hiring for us, Juanito? Maybe you'll have better luck."

But he didn't accept her challenge to take more interest in the place. "Got other plans . . ."

Something made her ask, "And do those plans include Maggie Ryerson?"

But he walked away without replying.

That afternoon she heard loud voices from the living quarters upstairs. Miguel was shouting at Juanito again. Miguel had been ill and should be conserving his strength, she well knew. She hurried to the foot of the stairs to try and overhear what the argument was about. But by then it was over.

Juanito came clumping down the stairs, his lips clamped. She asked what had happened upstairs, but he refused to discuss it.

It was a strange evening when darkness finally fell over Aleman's Barn. Heat lightning played in a distant cloud bank that hovered over the mountains yellowed by a full moon. Elnora was on edge, Miguel taciturn, still remaining deep within himself since his outburst with Juanito.

With the Hartleys gone she felt more and more uneasy in the big place, its store filled with sacks of flour, sugar, the shelves of tinned goods, counters piled high with yard goods, the dining room and saloon, the extensive rear yard, the area of junk, the corrals, surrounded by a gated stockade.

Juanito had disappeared sometime during the late afternoon. She supposed he had ridden off again, destination unknown, as usual. She had no idea when he would return. Jud Pryor was waiting on customers in the bar. Miguel, in a black mood, was talking to some ranchers.

After finishing the dishes, Elnora climbed the stairs. It had been a long day. Now that Dora Hartley was gone she had to do all the cooking, which was double now since the gold fields had opened up farther west. A stage coach stopped twice a day, using Aleman's Barn as a meal stop.

She undressed and got into bed. It seemed she had barely closed her eyes when a muffled gunshot came from the store that was directly below the living quarters. She sat bolt upright, sweeping back her long hair, her heart pounding. Moonlight through an open window touched the face of a French clock that had belonged to Luz, Miguel's first wife. It was three in the morning. She had been asleep for hours.

She could hear someone running downstairs.

Trembling, she got out of bed, slipped on a robe and dropped her revolver into a pocket as someone came up the stairs and began pounding on her door.

"Mrs. Aleman!" It was Jud Pryor's voice. And when she flung open the door, he said, "It's your husband, ma'am. He's been shot. He's asking for you."

"Oh, my God!"

She rushed down the stairs with Pryor. A night lamp burned in the dining room. The bar was dark, the customers having departed long ago.

She pushed open the heavy swing door that led to the store. Faint light from a lamp on a counter played over stacks of yard goods. Its yellow rim also fell on the figure crumpled on the floor. It was Miguel. There was an ugly stain across the front of the shirt she had laundered for him that very morning.

Chapter Sixteen

Lassiter restlessly paced his hotel room. He went to a window and stared out at the buildings of Juarez across the Rio, shimmering in the glow of a full moon. He thought of Bessie up in Denver and of Lola in Chihuahua City. And then as had happened so often in the weeks past, his mind did a complete turn to a vision of Maggie Ryerson taking his hand and saying, "Is this all I get . . . after last night?"

And there was Charlie Ryerson. What a challenge to devise some method of relieving the arrogant old bastard of some money. The two loves of Charlie Ryerson were his daughter and his money. And not always in that order, Lassiter had learned. It depended on the rancher's mood.

He blew a kiss in the direction of Ciudad Chihuahua, miles to the south, then got ready to check out of his hotel. Among his things he came across a letter Miguel had written him some weeks ago, meantioning the old bullet wound in his leg that had flared up. He also wrote that Juanito had been acting odd, almost furtive, which was no news. Miguel was obviously hinting for him to make another visit to try and straighten Juanito out. Lassiter was through playing blood brother. But he would stop by and try and cheer up Miguel and in the meantime make plans for the Ryersons, father and daughter. It stimulated him far more than a reunion in Chihuahua. Lola could wait.

He caught the evening westbound, bringing his

Winchester, a change of clothing, and some cash in a money belt. As the train screeched on curves and rattled on straight track he found his proposed project more rewarding than sleep. He'd already sampled the delights of Maggie, so he tucked her warmly away in a far corner of his mind and concentrated on the father. How to extract money from Charlie Ryerson, payment for misery the man had brought not only to his employees but to the residents of Banner County in general. He wondered if Ryerson was a good poker player. The man's arrogance would let him settle for nothing short of perfection in any field whether politics, cattle or cards. Lassiter smiled to himself in the dim coach lights. Smoke from the locomotive streamed past his window. He fell asleep thinking pleasantly of the Ryersons who would temporarily occupy his future but in different ways.

He was up early to the conductor's call of "Waverly . . . Waverly Junction!"

Lassiter nodded his thanks that the conductor had remembered to let him off at the flagstop. Several times before, he had disembarked here and picked up a horse from a trader for the ride west to Aleman's Barn.

This time the mustached horse trader greeted him with tragic news. "You heard about your friend, Miguel Aleman?"

Lassiter felt a premonition. "What's happened?"

"He's dead."

"Jesus Christ! Dead?" Lassiter took a moment to recover, shook his head and sighed deeply. Probably infection from the old leg wound had done Miguel in at last. Either that or it was worry of the no good foster son.

The horse trader's next words spun Lassiter around

from an inspection of a long-legged roan that interested him.

"Aleman was kilt by his own son."

"You mean Juanito?"

"Yep." The horse trader spat tobacco juice on the pulverized horse droppings that carpeted his trading lot. "When a Mex turns bad, he turns bad all the way."

Lassiter didn't bother to correct the stupidity. "You sure about Juanito?"

"What they say. He done it sure." The horse trader was enjoying his role as purveyor of startling news. "That ain't the worst of it," he went on, drawing out the moment. "Juanito's not only kilt his pa. He also murdered Charlie Ryerson's daughter."

This time Lassiter felt the shock to his heels. He groped for words, but could sort nothing out of his spinning mind.

"Hear that Sheriff Lambert an' a big posse pounded through last night about ten miles west of here," the horse trader said. "Sheriff figures Juanito is tryin' to get into Mexico."

Lassiter's mouth dried. Juanito no doubt heading for the Escobar rancho across the border, where Lassiter had tried to get him to go following the jail break. At least he'd know where to find the son-of-a-bitch when it came time to extract payment for what appeared to be cold blooded murder.

But before he went off half-cocked he'd see what Miguel's widow had to say, to be sure how much was fact, how much was rumor. Lassiter didn't even take time to dicker with the horse trader as usual, but purchased horse and saddle outright.

He booted his Winchester, strapped on his gear and

put the untested roan at a hard run to cover the miles to Aleman's Barn. For Juanito to murder his benefactor was one thing, but to kill Maggie Ryerson . . . It sickened Lassiter. A beautiful young girl overflowing with energy and love of life.

It can't be true, he kept telling himself as he settled down to the pattern of jolting miles. He shouted it into the wind that was whipping his eyes from the fast pace set by the roan. The gossiping horse trader didn't know what he was talking about. A lonely man in a lonely outpost seizing on a morsel of fact and letting his imagination run riot on the rest of it.

But when he stopped at midday to rest his weary horse he learned that the whole countryside between Aleman's Barn and the border was aroused over the brutal murders.

Even though it was out of his jurisdiction, Tod Lambert had indeed led a posse toward Mexico, taking the straightest route. But they hadn't been able to pick up any sign of the fleeing Juanito Aleman, so Lassiter was told. Someone said that Apache trackers were going to be brought in.

"It isn't true about the Ryerson girl," Lassiter said, dreading confirmation.

His informant nodded. "Juanito murdered her, no doubt. Blood stains was found on the ranch road. She ain't been seen since."

Lassiter chewed the last of a meat sandwich he'd bought for his noon meal. It lay on his stomach like a musket ball as he pushed westward again, then swinging north.

He was convinced Elnora Aleman could furnish answers to the macabre series of events. The thought that the lady herself might be a part of it streaked coldly through his mind. From the first his feelings toward her had been ambivalent.

During the long ride through the hills, across seemingly endless flats, he kept one eye open for posse dust. He could imagine Sheriff Lambert's wrath if he came face to face with the man who not only had humiliated him in his own jail, but had compounded it by freeing the very man now accused of double murder.

It was late afternoon when he got his first glimpse of the unpainted plank walls of Aleman's Barn and behind it the low backdrop of hills and the more distant mountains lost in the haze of fall heat.

He had expected the place to be crowded with mourners come to pay their respects to a Banner County pioneer. There were, however, only four horses at the hitch rack on the east west road. He wondered if Aleman's Barn was being shunned because of the Ryerson girl's murder. Perhaps Miguel's widow was being held accountable for the crimes of a stepson.

She heard the horse coming at a hard run, jerked aside a window curtain and then flung open the door. She hurled herself into his arms just as he slid wearily from the saddle. He felt her body curve against his, there in the front of the building.

"My prayers are truly answered," she sobbed. "I knew Miguel had written you weeks ago, but . . . Oh, God, it's terrible, terrible. Poor Miguel." She trembled, clutching at him so that he was even more aware of breasts and hips, pleasures that Miguel would never know again.

He tilted his chin against Elnora's soft hair and noticed that a man had come to the open doorway, wiping his hands on a bar rag. Sandy-haired and with a smile that strained to be friendly. Elnora stood with her back to the door, still clinging to Lassiter.

"Juanito . . . didn't . . . do it, Lassiter." Her tears dampened the front of his dusty shirt.

"Everybody says Juanito is a murderer for sure this time," he said.

"No, no. Miguel was still alive when Juanito left. He didn't want Miguel to know where he was going . . ."

Lassiter had returned more for Margaret Ryerson than Miguel, who had already had a life. It was to avenge the death of a young girl. He spoke softly against her hair. "They say he murdered Maggie Ryerson."

"Never. Lassiter, I tell you something in confidence . . ."

"Better hold it," he warned quietly.

The sandy-haired man still stood in the doorway, several feet away, wiping his hands, that damnable smile on his lips. Where had he seen that smile before?

"Jud and I turned the place upside down, hunting for the note Juanito left for me . . ."

"Jud?"

"I'm Jud," the man said pleasantly. "Guess she was so upset she forgot about me."

Elnora whirled around, wiping her eyes. "Jud, it's Lassiter. Isn't it wonderful that he's come!" Elnora exclaimed a little too heartily. And Lassiter had a feeling that Jud didn't think his arrival was all that wonderful.

Jud stuffed the bar rag in a pocket and stepped from the doorway to offer his hand. "Pryor's the name. Jud Pryor."

Lassiter accepted the hand. Its clasp was firm and hearty. There was still something vaguely familiar about the man.

"I'll get back and tend to my customers, Mrs. Aleman." He gave Lassiter a nod and returned to the bar. He did not close the door.

"Miguel hired Jud to help out here," Elnora said in answer to Lassiter's question.

"I see. Where's Miguel's body?"

"We buried him this morning," she said sadly. "Miguel had told me that when his time came he wanted no religious ceremony."

Lassiter nodded, watching the doorway. Miguel had once told him the same thing, feeling unworthy, probably, because of his part in the grim business of Juanito's parents.

There were three men at the bar, Lassiter noticed as he entered the building through the dining room. Two of the men turned to look at him through the archway between dining room and bar. They had the hard-planed look of men who earned their keep by their wits and possibly their guns. The third man stood with his back turned, hunched to one side as if in pain. This one, wearing an old striped silk shirt, did not look around.

"Who are they?" Lassiter asked Elnora in a low voice, as they moved toward the kitchen over a floor still damp from a fresh scrubbing.

"Two of them used to work for XR, so Jud told me a few minutes ago."

"And the other one?"

"Some stranger, I guess. Why?"

"The other two looked me over. He didn't. Just wondered why he wasn't curious."

"Let's take some coffee outside. I'll show you Miguel's grave." Elnora filled two cups from the big pot always on the back of the stove. Her hand trembled, he noticed. She still had her looks but there were signs of weariness around the eyes and at the corners of the mouth.

"Tell me about that note you said Juanito left," he ordered in a hoarse whisper. He shifted his Winchester under his arm, standing so he could watch the doorway to the bar. The men had returned to their drinking.

"You sound skeptical," she said, "about the note." She gestured at a bulky apron that always hung on a nail when she wasn't using it. "Juanito left it in my apron pocket. I read it, returned it. And then the next thing I knew it was missing."

They carried their coffee cups into the store because Lassiter wanted to see where Miguel had been shot. He stared at the bloodstains on the floor, then jerked his head. "Let's go outside."

As they crossed the yard, he wondered about this handsome widow. "When you found Miguel, was he still alive?"

"No . . . He was dead."

He frowned. He helped her over some loose bricks. They skirted the big upended wagon where he had saved her life. He opened the heavy gate and blocked it so they could get back in. Miguel's grave was on a knoll. His name had been cut in a plain wooden cross, and the date of his death. She didn't know the year of his birth. Juanito had not been here to tell her, even if he knew.

"Jud made the cross for me," she said. A lock of red-gold hair had come unpinned. She brushed it aside.

"This Jud your handyman . . . all the way?"

She looked up at him, her eyes bright with anger. "It isn't as you seem to think. Miguel liked him . . ."

"And you . . . ?"

"Jud has been something to lean on in this terrible time . . . to a point."

"Jud moved into Miguel's shoes?"

She shook her head, said defiantly, "Nor will any man until a decent period of mourning has passed."

"Your friend Jud doesn't look the type to wait very long. How'd Miguel come to hire him?" He set his coffee cup on a stump and watched the many narrow windows of Aleman's Barn.

She was speaking of an evening when some of their horses had either been let out accidentally or were stolen. "There were supposed to be rustlers in the area. Miguel's leg had been bothering him and I didn't want him to go after the horses and possibly come up against those rustlers."

"And where the hell was Juanito when all this happened?"

"Away. Probably seeing the Ryerson girl. I suspected he's been seeing her on the sly for a long time."

"Hmmmm."

"To make a long story short, Jud brought the horses back. He'd found them wandering loose."

"Convenient."

"He didn't have to return them."

Lassiter frowned at the grave then looked at the low hills where he had killed Chick Kelleray and friend. And later killed the third one, Sawbridge, up on the mountain. And the killing wasn't over yet. He knew it now. He faced the building again. Elnora rubbed her forearms, shuddering.

"I . . . I have the strangest feeling that we're being watched."

"I'm keeping my eyes open. This Jud of yours reminds me of somebody."

"I have the same feeling."

"I'm waiting patiently, Elnora," he said through his teeth. "The note."

"I've told no one . . . I just didn't know what to do."

"But the note Juanito left you is missing. So somebody's read it. What the hell did it say?"

"Don't yell at me . . ." Her lower lip trembled and he braced himself. He was tired and distraught and all twisted up inside by the grim day.

"He and Maggie are eloping. He's going to the Ober Hills. There's a gold strike there. He's going to try and make a stake so he and Maggie can make a new life. Away from her father. Away from Miguel. Of course when he left me the note he didn't realize Miguel would be dead within a few hours." She looked at the ground for a moment, her eyes squeezed shut. "He wanted me to break the news to Miguel gently as I could. If Miguel took it too hard, then I was to get word to him at Ober Hills. I didn't find the note until the next morning after . . . after Miguel was shot. When I went to put on my apron . . ." Her voice trailed away. She looked up at him. "I didn't want to talk about the note where Jud could overhear and I . . . I just had this strange feeling that someone was watching us and might overhear."

"Then you don't trust him all the way."

"He's been very kind, helpful. But there's one thing . . ."

"Talk. Nobody's going to hear us out here."

"When he came upstairs night before last and told me Miguel had been shot, he said Miguel was asking for me . . ." She broke off, drawing a deep breath. "And as we were going downstairs together, he said Miguel accused Juanito of shooting him. And when I got there Miguel was dead. I just feel he never knew what hit him, that he didn't speak at all. Just a hunch I guess."

"Hunches sometimes pay off."

"And then the next morning when I managed to get breakfast and found the note . . . well, I got to thinking."

He tried to weigh sincerity against the possibility that she was a very good actress. So Juanito, if Elnora could be believed that is, was on the way to the Ober Hills with Maggie. Lassiter felt a faint stir of jealousy which he instantly shrugged aside. This was no time for that, he told himself.

"Talk about hunches, I've got one that your friend Jud saw you reading that note. He watched his chance and stole it out of your apron pocket."

"Don't keep calling him my friend. You being here has helped set my thinking straight in a lot of ways. Yes, I do believe you're right and I'm worried."

"You talk to anybody about the note? Tell the sheriff?"

"I didn't know what to do, frankly. I . . . I didn't want to see them go pounding after Juanito and . . . and kill him before Maggie could even explain."

"Another hunch. Jud sent them off on a wild goose chase to the border."

"Yes. He told Sheriff Lambert he'd seen Juanito head that way."

"Jud knows where Juanito and the girl have gone. And he's got some game of his own, you can bet on that."

"But what could it be?"

"Still got your gun?"

"Yes, but . . ."

"I haven't time to deal with Jud now. You pretend nothing's happened. But stay away from him. Lock yourself in your room. I'm going after Juanito and. . . ." he gave her a twisted smile . . . "his bride-to-be."

"Be careful, Lassiter."

"Do my damndest to find Juanito before something happens . . ."

"To escape the gallows once and then having the threat over his head again." Elnora shuddered.

"This time they won't bother with a gallows." He watched her from a corner of his eye. "Who do you think killed Miguel?"

"At first I assumed it was those rustlers that Miguel surprised. Or someone trying to rob the store . . ."

"Your friend Jud's the one."

She looked startled. "I may have my doubts about him but I don't think he'd commit murder. Those men in the bar are the type who could. It makes me nervous just being around them."

"Jud brings back horses Miguel thinks were rustled. Miguel hires him. Too pat. And just why would Juanito leave a note for you and not for Miguel?"

"I told you. He wanted me to break the news about the elopement. And he told me where he was going so if it was too much of a shock, I could send somebody after him. He worried that Miguel might take it too hard. Of course he would have no idea that Miguel was already dead by the time I found the note."

"So you said . . ."

She glanced at the building a little apprehensively. "Here's something else."

"Tell me," he said, watching for movement at the windows.

"Juanito left in a wagon. One of the wagons is missing. Jud hasn't been here long enough to notice. And Juanito took Miguel's old tent and bedding and cooking utensils."

"Take their time and enjoy the trip, I guess," Lassiter said thinly, a stir of jealousy intruding on his relief that Maggie was apparently alive, not murdered as he and most everyone else had been led to believe. And was it really any of his business if Maggie wanted a honeymoon before a wedding?

He knew Sheriff Lambert and the posse were hunting for tracks left by a single rider, not realizing the man they sought was traveling in a wagon. And heading not south toward the border but west and north to the Ober Hills.

"Here's the way I got it figured," Lassiter said. "I think Pryor might have seen Juanito and Maggie leave in the wagon. He found the note Juanito left for you. He saw a chance to get Miguel out of the way and blame it onto Juanito. Then lie about Maggie."

She put a hand to her forehead. "That horrible possibility occurred to me. But I just couldn't . . . believe it."

"Believe it now." He studied the big rambling unpainted structure through the open gate in the stockade but saw no sign of Pryor. "Tell me, how did word get to the sheriff? A long ride up to the county seat."

"Lambert was south of here at a ranch on a tax matter, I understand. Pryor got word to him. I hear Lambert formed a posse of every ranch hand he could find and roared off for Mexico."

"Without even stopping to wonder about it . . ." He broke off, suddenly aware of the sounds of horses and a wagon coming from the south.

Elnora rushed with him to a store window that overlooked the road. A middle aged couple were squeezed together on the seat of a Texas hack wagon. Two younger riders suffered its dust.

"The Morrisons," Elnora breathed. "I was told they'd be coming."

Lassiter made a decision. "Stick with the woman,"

he told Elnora. "When they leave, go with them. Make up some excuse about you having to get away for a spell. Because of Miguel being murdered here."

Mention of the macabre incident caused her to shudder. "What about Pryor?" she asked anxiously, glancing toward the barroom.

"I'll handle him when I get back," he said in a low voice. "But for now you'll be out of the way. Do as I say, Elnora."

"You were suspicious of me at first, weren't you?"

"Hell no."

"Liar," she said brokenly. "It hurt to think you'd believe I could have had a hand in it." Her eyes misted. "Come back to me, Lassiter."

His look was sardonic. "I'll be back, one way or another. If I'm in a pine box, celebrate with a wake. Get drunk, then find yourself a good man."

"Don't talk like that . . ."

He got her by an arm and marched her into the dining room just as the Morrisons were alighting from the wagon, their two sons dismounting.

The three men who had been drinking at the bar took that moment to head out the saloon door to their horses. Lassiter tried to see the face of the one in the striped silk shirt who moved as if in pain. But when the man mounted, the other two were quickly behind him as if to block Lassiter's view. They spun their horses away from the rack and rode east at a canter.

Lassiter found Jud Pryor staring at him through the archway. "Your friends left in a hurry," Lassiter said.

"Guess they figured to try and collect the *re*-ward. I hear the county's offering five thousand dollars."

Lassiter groaned inwardly; a chance for some hot head to kill an innocent man and earn bounty money.

Martha Morrison, a greying, heavyset woman waddled into the dining room. "Heard about your husband, Mrs. Aleman," she said stiffly. "Only decent to come by and pay our respects."

Lassiter recognized obvious dislike in the woman's tone. He whispered, "Don't forget what I told you," and ducked out the rear door. He crossed the littered yard.

There in the nearest corral he roped out a fresh horse and switched saddles. He could hear a drone of voices from inside. He glimpsed Pryor serving a drink to the husband, bringing it from the bar to the dining room. He didn't expect trouble from Pryor as long as the Morrisons and their two husky sons were there.

It was imperative that he find Juanito and the girl as quickly as possible. Things were beginning to add up for as the three men had left the bar, something clicked in his mind. He hadn't been able to get a look at the face of the man who walked hunched over. But he sensed who he was. It didn't come to him until they were riding away.

Freddie Peal, hired by shirttail kin to cripple Lassiter; the sole survivor of the trio who had tried to jump him out of Denver. Peal still suffering from the glancing blow from a foreleg of Lassiter's lunging horse.

Lassiter had also, belatedly, tied in Jud Pryor to the dirty business. Pryor's smile had puzzled him. More of a smirk than smile. He suddenly remembered where he had seen it before.

He rode through the gate, glanced at Miguel's grave.

"I worked one miracle for Juanito," he said to the mound of earth. "I don't know about another one. But I'll do my damndest."

Following the dust of Peal and the other two was

easy. They rode east for half a mile or so, as if to throw off anyone who might be watching them, then doubled back, angling west and north. The Ober Hills, scene of a gold strike, lay in that general direction. The direction taken by Juanito and Maggie, if Elnora could be believed.

It wasn't long before everything was turned around. For two miles or more he had been paralleling Peal and the other two, using a dense tangle of mesquite as a screen. They were about a quarter of a mile north of him and an equal distance ahead.

He was trying to keep them in sight when a voice boomed out suddenly from behind him.

"Right through the back of the head, Lassiter! If you don't pull up that horse!"

He recognized the voice with a shock, as belonging to someone who on this, of all days, he didn't want to encounter. He reined in, glanced over his shoulder. Charlie Ryerson, looking as if he'd shed twenty pounds, was astride a big bay horse on a trail that cut through the mesquite. The cattleman held a cocked rifle. Behind him and slightly to one side was his foreman, the bearded Hal Dempster.

"You better listen to me, Ryerson," Lassiter urged. "I know something . . ."

"I might have known you were in on it!" Ryerson interrupted with a snarl. "Sit right where you are or I'll put a bullet in your head. I'd rather see you hang for having a hand in kidnaping my daughter, but . . ."

"*Kidnaping?* You're a fool, Ryerson. Listen to me . . ."

At Aleman's Barn, Jud Pryor said, "Can I see you for a minute, Mrs. Aleman?"

It was just after Elnora had noticed, with relief, that Lassiter had ridden away. She detached herself from

Mrs. Morrison. Mr. Morrison, rail thin, had finished his drink and stood stiffly beside his two husky sons in the dining room.

It was plain to Elnora that it was the woman who had dragged them here. The icy Mrs. Morrison offering condolences. A woman with a deep sense of propriety, that overrode her dislike for the too-young, too-attractive Aleman widow.

Elnora entered the saloon, empty save for Pryor behind the bar. "What is it, Jud?" she asked, trying to keep a burgeoning fear from showing in her voice.

"You thank the woman for coming," he said softly. "But don't move one inch from where you're standing. If you do, I'll kill the woman."

Elnora shivered at the cold threat. She glanced down at the rifle muzzle resting at the back edge of the bar where it wouldn't be noticed by the Morrisons in the dining room. She looked at Jud Pryor's thinned hazel eyes and knew he meant what he said.

"Thank you for coming, Mrs. Morrison," she managed without collapsing. "You and your husband and your sons. But I'm very tired . . ." She let it hang there. They were glad for an excuse to leave.

As they were going out the door, Pryor said loudly, so they could overhear, "I've worked with Mexicans. Sooner or later that bad blood shows up. Like it did in Juanito."

"It doesn't apply . . ." Elnora began shakily.

"You mean that crazy story that he isn't even Mex?"

"Even if he were, it still doesn't apply. You condemn a person with . . . without even giving him a chance."

Pryor seemed amused. He bared his teeth, lowered his voice. "As you've probably been condemned yourself, dear lady, more than once."

Elnora had an urge to scream at the Morrisons, but

Pryor had shifted to a window, the deadly rifle covering the woman as she climbed heavily into the wagon.

"Jud, you're fired!" she cried, when the wagon pulled away. "Get *out*!"

Futile rage as she well knew, but something she had been compelled to say. He laughed at her. The Morrisons were hurrying off down the road, heading toward their ranch.

"My poor brother tried to get a toehold in this Banner County," Pryor said coldly. "He died trying. I'm going to make it. I figured you couldn't run Aleman's Barn alone. You'd need me . . . maybe even as a husband," a smirk stamped to his lips.

"You're insane to think I'd ever marry you!"

"It was in your eyes one night. But then you had to go and say you were loyal to your husband."

"If I had any weakness toward you it lasted for only a moment. I recovered quickly."

"Lassiter turned you against me," he accused.

"I already had my suspicions . . ."

"I planned to finish everything right here. With you in on it with me . . . if you didn't balk. But now Lassiter's loose and I've got to change those plans. And maybe you're just too much to put up with . . ."

She gasped as he lazily pointed the rifle in her direction.

Chapter Seventeen

Lassiter talked long and earnestly into the muzzle of a carbine aimed at his face. A lizard scampered along the bed of a dry creek bisected by the narrow trail through the wall of mesquite. Color slowly drained from Ryerson's haggard face. The cocked rifle was unwavering in his puffy hands.

"I don't believe a damn word you said!" Ryerson cried, when Lassiter finished laying out the facts as he knew them. "Maggie wouldn't elope with that son-of-a-bitch. He kidnaped her."

"We're wasting time. Their lives are in danger!"

"I knew from the first that she wasn't dead. Juanito spread that story about blood being found on the ranch road . . . her blood."

"Believe what I'm trying to tell you, Ryerson!"

Ryerson jerked his head at the foreman on a dappled gray behind him on the trail. "Dempster, show him the ransom note. It's in my coat pocket. I want both my hands on this rifle!"

Ryerson kept the rifle level. Dempster rode up beside him and slipped a hand in the pocket of a corduroy jacket. He drew out a folded paper and started riding toward Lassiter.

"Be careful of him," Ryerson warned. "He's tricky. Make sure he gets hold of the ransom note, and not your wrist."

"I won't get too close," Hal Dempster said nervously.

He licked his lips and did as he was told. He then reined aside, waiting. Sweat poured off his face.

Lassiter scanned the ransom note printed in block letters, even the signature. It demanded fifty thousand dollars for the return of Margaret Ryerson. Ryerson was to confide in no one but his foreman. He was to come by Aleman's Barn, pick up Elnora Aleman and bring her and the money to Tejano Lake. There his daughter would be returned to him. It was to be today, in the late afternoon.

Lassiter held his breath and waved the ransom note at Dempster, hoping this time the foreman would be careless. But Dempster made no attempt to pluck the note from Lassiter's fingers. He didn't move. Lassiter let the piece of paper flutter to the sandy ground.

"Fifty thousand dollars," Lassiter breathed, eyeing one end of a brown leather satchel lashed to the cantle that he could see projecting from behind Ryerson's bulk.

"Could only raise twenty-five," Ryerson said, "on such short notice. Disappointed, Lassiter?"

Dempster had turned in the saddle to frown at his employer. "But . . . the note said fifty . . ." Lassiter noticed that the man paled at Ryerson's next words.

"But twenty-five thousand will be enough to get that greedy Juanito excited. Then I'll kill him. Kill anybody else who's in on it with him. Including you, Lassiter."

"Somebody's playing you for a fool, Ryerson!" Lassiter shouted, keeping one eye on the rifle, hoping to see it waver. It didn't.

"Maybe her predicament is some of her own doing," Ryerson said, his voice shaking. "I've suspected she started seeing Juanito again on the sly."

Lassiter's heart slowly thumped as he stared down the cold eye of the rifle muzzle. He raised his voice. "I tell you again and you listen! Your daughter and Juanito are going to be *married*! It's her happiness you're going to ruin . . ."

"You call this happiness?" Ryerson screamed at him. "*This!* Dempster, show him the clothes!"

Dempster seemed unsure of himself but removed some tattered garments from his saddlebag and held them up for Lassiter's inspection. Lassiter recognized the remains of a beige blouse, a divided skirt. He kept his face straight.

Ryerson's grip tightened on the rifle. "Dempster found those on the ranch road. Where that fiend waylaid my daughter and stripped off her clothing . . ."

"Those clothes were torn weeks ago," Lassiter cut in, keeping his voice level, despite the strain.

"Liar! Tell him, Dempster. You saw her wearing those same clothes the morning she disappeared."

"Yeah, yeah, that's right," Dempster mumbled.

Lassiter shook his head, gambling for time. Dempster was fidgeting in the saddle, reaching around for a black-handled gun at his belt. He froze as Lassiter spoke.

"Like I already told you, Ryerson, the clothes were torn weeks ago. When she was supposed to have spent the night in Brightwater with a girl named Jennifer."

"How the hell would *you* know!" Ryerson cried.

"Main thing is, Dempster lied! He's in on the kidnaping . . ."

Dempster finished his reach for the black handled gun as Lassiter was already slamming in the spurs. Lassiter's horse leaped, crashing into Ryerson's mount. Force of the collision discharged the rifle into the air. Dempster's bullet drilled into a bank of the dry creek, spewing sand. It was his one and only chance, for he was smashed from the saddle, doubled up from the .44

slug that ripped into him an inch above the belt buckle.

Before a stunned Ryerson could recover and steady his own horse, Lassiter twisted the rifle out of his grasp. He aimed it at Dempster, who lay on his back, both hands pressed against an ugly stomach wound.

"Tell him, Dempster! Tell him you were in on it from the start!"

"Ed . . . Ed said it'd be easy . . ."

"Ed Covey, yeah. Chick Kelleray's half brother!"

Ryerson looked at him in surprise. Lassiter did not return the rifle. He said coldly, "We've got some lives to save. We don't have one damned minute to spare."

"Dempster," Ryerson breathed, looking down at blood leaking through the man's fingers. "I thought it strange the note said confide in no one but him. But I supposed it was because Juanito thought I should have a bodyguard with all that money." Ryerson sagged in the saddle, but had enough strength left to swear at the dying man on the ground. "Made you foreman . . . no loyalty . . . none at all."

"He'll die here. We can't waste time with him. Ryerson, you lead the way."

They started riding. Dempster's horse was running loose across the flats. There was no time to run it down. No longer did Lassiter concern himself with the three men he had been trailing when Ryerson jumped him. If they got in his way, they were dead. What lay ahead at Tajano Lake was what concerned him now.

"My guess is all along they planned to take your money," Lassiter said to Ryerson's back, "then kill you. Blame it on Juanito."

They were heading toward Tejano Lake that Lassiter recalled as being west of Aleman's Barn.

"Dempster swore he'd seen Maggie wearing those

clothes the morning she disappeared!" Ryerson shouted back at him. "I believed him!"

"He lied. You know it now."

"When this is over, I am going to kill you, Lassiter!"

"Maybe you'll try. Others have."

"If what you say is true about those clothes, then you raped my daughter. I thought there was something strange about that night. Maggie didn't spend it in Brightwater. But she'd never talk about it."

"Ryerson, I didn't harm Maggie." Their horses skirted the base of a hill, clattered over a hundred yards of hardpan, then reached sand again. "I think a lot of Maggie," Lassiter continued. "And if you have one ounce of love for your daughter, keep shut about those torn clothes. Something a future husband doesn't need to know."

They rode a mile, two miles, cutting toward Tejano Creek which fed the lake. Lassiter straining his eyes to try and catch sight of Freddie Peal and the other two. He told Ryerson about Peal and the two former XR riders who had teamed up with him.

"No loyalty," muttered Ryerson again, shaking his head. "Can I have my rifle?"

"Maybe later. Keep riding." Lassiter ached from weariness, the long hours in the saddle from Waverly, the day of tension, of danger. Everything had turned completely around, from double murder to elopment and now kidnaping. He had suspected Elnora of having a hand in it, then changed his mind. He hoped by now she was safely with the Morrisons.

He tried to recall what he knew of Tejano Lake. Not really a lake but a large pool in a rock basin, formed by Tejano Creek before it disappeared underground. Indians had used it as a campground. Also men on the dodge from both sides of the border.

As they approached, keeping their horses to a walk now, Lassiter kept scanning the ground for sign of Peal and his two friends. It puzzled him that there was no fresh sign.

Now and then when he heard the clink of gold coins shifting in the satchel tied to Ryerson's saddle, he thought of how easy it would be to relieve the old bastard of his money. Had it not been for Juanito and the girl.

Ryerson looked around at him. "Let me have my rifle."

"You threatened to kill me, remember," Lassiter said with a twisted smile.

"When Maggie's safe, I'll face you, man to man."

"Hell with that. Whether I want to or not, I've got to take a chance on you." He rode up and thrust the rifle back into the rancher's hands. "From here on out, keep your eyes open. And remember one thing. Don't give these bastards an inch. Shoot to kill. They figured to murder your daughter and Juanito the minute they got their hands on that money. Murder you."

Ryerson's haggard face was streaked with sweat and dust. "I believe you." Then he drew a deep breath, his mouth set. "But she'll never marry Juanito . . . *never*!"

"Ride ahead of me," Lassiter ordered. "I still don't trust you at my back." When Ryerson started cursing Juanito, Lassiter reminded him coldly of the murder of two drifters years back. "You've been running from it since. Taking it out on your daughter and everybody else."

Ryerson muttered something. Patches of moisture darkened the collar of his jacket. A late sun suddenly slid under a cloud, throwing shadows across the face of low hills. Tejano Lake lay less than a mile ahead. Wherever possible Lassiter directed them away from dried brush and onto sand to muffle hoofbeats. Finally he picked up a faint sound of water rushing downhill and knew it was Tejano Creek spilling over a downslope of rocks and into the lake. The sound increased. Hopefully it would help cover their approach.

Ryerson was first to reach a lip of rock at a cliff edge, Lassiter slightly behind him. Lassiter crowded in, pulling up his horse, and took everything in at a glance. Twenty feet below was a camp at the edge of an expanse of blue water that shimmered in the sunlight. A rainbow mist rose from the creek as it spilled into the lake. Juanito, head drooping to one side, was on the ground, arms lashed to the wheel of a wagon. He looked as if he had been beaten. Four horses were tied to a cottonwood. Lassiter glimpsed a small tent near one of three twenty foot walls of rock that surrounded the lake, really a large pool, on three sides.

Two men were lounging on a blanket in front of the tent, playing cards. Rifles were within reach. Lassiter had never seen them before.

"You take the black-haired one," Lassiter whispered, cocking his Winchester. "I'll get his friend . . ."

But Ryerson was too overcome with emotion. He pointed at the tent twenty feet below and screamed, *"Maggie!"*

The two men bounded from the blanket, scattering cards, their rifles swinging up. Lassiter wasted no time on fancy shooting but tried to aim for the widest part of each body. The first man, with long curling black hair, crumpled soundlessly. His stocky companion, wearing a red kerchief, lunged for the tent. No wide target presented this time. A shot through the skull spilled him before he could open the tent flaps. Echoes from the rifle shots, blended as one, reverberated from the rock walls. As Lassiter sent his horse down a steep trail, his eyes sweeping the campsite for more of the enemy, he saw Maggie claw her way out of the tent flaps that had been tied together.

She ran, not toward him or her father, midway down the steep trail, but to Juanito. She snatched up a knife that lay beside a dead campfire and rushed to the wagon. She knelt and began to saw at the lashing that bound him to a wheel.

"Lassiter," Juanito managed through swollen lips.

Maggie cut through the last rope, whipped around on her heels to look up at Lassiter. One of her cheeks was puffy, there was a rent in her blue shirt. Her Levis were dusty, one knee ripped. They looked like the clothes he had bought her that momentous morning in Kendall Springs. But he couldn't be sure.

He jerked his rifle at the two dead men. "Anybody else around?"

She seemed mute, either with fear or some other emotion. She barely looked at her father.

Juanito answered for her. "Nobody . . . else . . . now . . ." His face was bloodied, one eye swollen shut. He seemed barely able to stand.

Lassiter didn't bother with the man wearing the red kerchief who had died instantly. His black-haired companion was in bad shape. Lassiter stood over him.

"Three men I followed for a ways. Freddie Peal and two others. Where are they?"

"Reckon Monagal shack . . . pick up gear there. Then come here . . ." his voice trailed away.

Ryerson had dismounted. He stared at the two men, one dead, one on the edge. "*You,*" he said to them and Lassiter gathered that they were former XR riders. Lassiter turned to Ryerson and barked orders.

"Get your daughter and Juanito out of here." He

flung a hand in the direction of a level trail on that side of Tejano Lake not blocked by a rock wall. "Do it *now!*"

Ryerson tried to get his daughter by the arm, but she sidestepped him and came to Lassiter. She looked up into his eyes, questioningly. And he knew what bothered her. Despite her harrowing experience, with death only a whisper away for them all, she needed to be reassured about a certain night in the mountains. He shook his head, giving her a tight smile that indicated, he hoped, that she was not to worry. His lips were sealed.

With the emotional moment past, he gave Ryerson a shove. "Do what I told you! Damn it, *move!*" He gestured toward saddle horses that had belonged to the pair of guards.

"What will you do, Lassiter?" Maggie asked tensely.

"A little surprise party for whoever comes here . . ."

Juanito said, "I'm staying with Lassiter," the speech slurred because of the mangled lips. "Time I stood by him." He tried to push Maggie toward her father who stood woodenly staring at a daughter who had barely looked at him.

"Juanito, don't be a damn fool!" Lassiter yelled at him. "Clear out."

"I can use a rifle," Maggie said. "Maybe it's better to surprise them here than risk having them trap us later."

But the choice was not theirs to make.

Jud Pryor appeared suddenly on the rim where Lassiter himself had been only minutes before. He was on foot, pointing a rifle down at a slender figure near the pool that was now in deeper shadow. Maggie directly in the sights of his rifle.

At Pryor's side was Freddie Peal, also afoot. He was hunched over from the pain of ribs obviously unhealed, broken or badly cracked. A lure of gold outweighing pain and the time consumed in seeking medical attention.

Pryor spoke in a loud, confident voice. "Lassiter, bring the satchel of money. Come alone or I'll kill the girl. Killing a female wouldn't bother me any more than peeling a fingernail."

Lassiter swallowed, his mind racing. On Pryor's lips was the smirk so reminiscent of the late Chick Kelleray.

"Don't do it, Lassiter!" Maggie cried. "He'll kill you . . ."

"Of course I will, Miss Ryerson," Pryor called down in a drawling voice. "He murdered my brother. I was going to have to look him up, but he came to me instead."

Tears began to spill down Maggie's cheeks, dampening the one that was swollen as well as the one unmarked. "Haven't you killed enough already?"

"I'd rather save you for later, Miss Ryerson," he said, his voice taking on an edge, "but if you make trouble . . ." He let it hang there.

"Kill the lot of 'em, Ed!" Freddie Peal screamed.

"It's Pryor now, Freddie. Jud Pryor. Hell, I figure to be a power here in Banner County. You coming, Lassiter, or do I kill that girl!"

"I'm coming."

"And by the way, Lassiter," Pryor said, the smirk again on his lips, "disarm yourself. But carefully if you want to see the skull of that young lady intact."

Lassiter put down Winchester and .44 while Maggie watched him in horror. Ryerson was ordered to drop the rifle he had been holding woodenly. Juanito tried to limp to Maggie's side but Pryor shouted for him to stay back.

Lassiter picked up the knife Maggie had used to free Juanito. He cut the satchel loose. How heavy it was, pleasantly so. But he had no time to dwell on that. His heartbeat swelled in his ears to minimize the sound of rushing water. He looked around, saw the horses standing placidly, tails switching. Tejano Lake was a blue eye in a socket of rock walls. Maggie was pale, but standing with shoulders back. Juanito seemed almost out on his feet from the beating he had received. Ryerson stood with his feet apart, staring at the dead man, the one killed instantly, the other who had succumbed seconds ago with a drumming of heels upon the ground. Ryerson looked as if accusing them of disloyalty even though no longer on his payroll. Unable to understand anyone in the world but himself. Or so Lassiter thought.

Lassiter took a final look at Maggie's stricken face. As he passed Ryerson, the rancher's lips moved.

But Lassiter did not turn his head. He looked at the two men up on the rim. He began his climb, the heavy satchel swinging at the end of a long arm. Up the slanting trail he'd ridden down only a short time before. His neck ached as he held his head back to keep his eyes locked on Pryor's face. At Pryor's side, Freddie Peal was muttering.

"His damn hoss like to tore me to pieces. Lemme shoot him now . . ."

"Shut up, Freddie," Pryor said, that identifying smile again pasted to his lips. "Be thankful you're kinfolk."

"Yeah, otherwise I'd be dead like them others." Peal gave a bark of nervous laughter. His greedy eyes were riveted on the satchel Lassiter was carrying up the path.

Lassiter sensed he knew what had happened to the other two men. Pryor felt he had the situation well in hand and no longer needed witnesses he couldn't trust. And why give them a cut of the money? Obviously the pair Lassiter had killed below at the lake would have also gone the same way. More horror would have swept the county; additional victims of that madman Juanito Aleman. Juanito killed, of course, by Pryor and his shirttail kin, Freddie Peal, while they were attempting to rescue that poor Ryerson girl. And Ryerson himself a victim along with his daughter. All for a brown satchel weighted down with gold coins.

"I think in view of everything," Pryor said to Peal as Lassiter neared the top of his climb, "that we forget Aleman's Barn and the rest of it. Fifty thousand American dollars will buy a lot of rancho in Mexico."

Lassiter seized on the opening Pryor had given him. "Ryerson couldn't raise fifty thousand," Lassiter said as he neared the lip of the brushy rock wall.

Pryor wasn't fooled. "That satchel looks heavy enough."

"Full of wagon bolts. Money's at Aleman's Barn."

Pryor leaned forward slightly to peer down at him. "Lassiter, you're a liar."

Lassiter shook his head. His boots crunched on pebbles that had spilled on the steep trail. He pretended to lose his balance for a moment so as to stall for time. The sun poked from behind a cloud for a last fling of day's warmth at Mother Earth. A horse below loudly broke wind and another cut loose with a gully washer. Life goes on, Lassiter thought grimly, as he started his climb again.

He began to taunt Pryor. "All this planning and killing for a bag full of bolts."

"I repeat, you are a goddamned liar." But a shred of uncertainty had crept into Pryor's voice. "Hurry it up, I want a look at that bag!"

Lassiter reached the top of the cliff and level ground. He pretended to be winded and stood spraddle-legged, breathing hard. Peal was a few feet away, hunched over, glaring at him. Then his gaze slipped hungrily to the bag Lassiter still held. Pryor snarled an oath.

"Put the bag down, then step back," he ordered.

Lassiter hesitated, every nerve screaming. As he had started toward the path, Ryerson had given him faint hope. A nod of the head, a muttered, "When you get close to him I'll grab my rifle."

If Ryerson was ever going to make his move it had to be now. While Pryor's attention was diverted from Maggie, standing stiffly below, and to Lassiter and the satchel of money still gripped in his right hand. Waning sun dried sweat on Lassiter's forehead. He could taste salt on his lips. His heartbeat was a war drum as he and Pryor locked eyes.

"Did you hear me!" Pryor shouted, gesturing with the rifle. "Put the bag down. Then back up to the edge of the cliff. Till your toes are on the edge. When your legs begin to shake, think of my brother, think of Chick. You got twenty feet to fall backwards, Lassiter. Your head will look like a melon dropped off a barn roof. *Move!*"

Peal uttered a sudden warning cry. "That fat one's grabbed a rifle!"

"Shoot him!"

Peal's rifle crashed. Its sudden blast of sound nearly washed out Ryerson's strangled cry from below.

In that same split second, Lassiter with both hands pitched the heavy satchel at Peal's lacerated rib cage. Peal screamed, his weapon slipped from his fingers and disappeared over the cliff edge. As the satchel hurtled from Lassiter's hands he lunged in the same movement. The fork of thumb and forefinger slammed at a Pryor wrist bone. He snapped the wrist upward with such force that Pryor lost his footing and his grip on the weapon. Before Lassiter could grab it, Pryor drew a revolver and fired. Lassiter felt the searing pain across the underside of the right upper arm as he followed through with his leap. He smashed with both clenched fists at the pistol in his fury. He jarred it loose. Pryor, backing up, reached under his shirt for another. Lassiter caught the front of the shirt, tearing it slightly. Still clinging to the shirt, he flung himself backward to the rocky ground, smashing down brush. One of his feet slammed into Pryor's midriff. Pryor uttered a screech of fear as he was catapulted into space.

Lassiter checked his own backward slide in the thick brush at the cliff edge. Pain and numbness spread along his right arm. He got to his feet. Pryor had screamed all the way down, having had time to think of what he had done, what he had lost.

Juanito had staggered over to pick up Ryerson's dropped carbine. He aimed it at Peal who was staggering around in his agony. The money satchel slamming into his ribcage had torn open the old wounds.

"Hold it, Juanito!" Lassiter yelled down, his voice weakening. "Let's save him for the gallows!"

Then he picked up Pryor's revolver with his left hand and herded a terrified Peal limping down the trail. Blood from an inch deep gash along the underside of the right arm darkened Lassiter's shirt and the sleeve.

When they reached level ground, Maggie was looking down at her father, then at Peal. "That man killed him."

Lassiter thought it proper to say, "I'm sorry."

"I . . . I guess I am," she said, numbly shaking her head. "Yes, I am sorry. After all, he was my father." She closed her eyes. She opened them, focused on Lassiter. She gave a low cry. "You're hurt . . ."

A dead man's shirt made a compress for the arm wound. After Peal was tied to a saddle, the three of them got the wagon team hitched up and Ryerson's body hoisted into the bed. Juanito had recovered sufficiently to drive the team.

"Lambert can claim the other bodies," Lassiter said through his teeth. "If the buzzards have left anything, that is."

Maggie, clinging to a seat brace, began talking about their experience. "We were halfway to the Ober Hills when they jumped us. How did they *know*?"

"Pryor read that note Juanito left for Elnora," Lassiter said.

"And you say Pryor murdered Miguel," Juanito said haltingly through lacerated lips. "And blamed me for it. Lassiter, if it hadn't been for you . . ." He turned the swollen face to Lassiter who rode beside the wagon, Peal ahead of him, head down.

Juanito said, "Miguel and I never understood each other. But . . . I guess I'll always think of him as my father. I had no chance to know my real one."

Lassiter swung close to Maggie. "Are you all right? Did they . . . harm you?"

She knew what he meant. "They didn't touch me. They planned to . . . when it was over." She shuddered, then turned to look him in the eye. "The only man I want is Juanito. You understand that, Lassiter?"

He didn't reply, only gave a slight nod of the head.

When they reached Aleman's Barn, Lassiter knew the day of tragedy was not yet over. He saw the sign on one of the doors. He spurred forward, noting no horses at the hitch racks, no wagons. His heart felt as if it pumped to a halt when he saw the neat lettering on the sign, the same fine block printing as had been on the ransom note.

> DUE TO THE DEATH OF THE OWNER, ALEMAN'S BARN WILL REMAIN CLOSED UNTIL NEXT WEEK.
>
> ELNORA ALEMAN

Lassiter swung down, his arm hurting, and yelled at Juanito just pulling up in the wagon. "Door's locked. A key, or we'll have to kick it in!"

Juanito limped forward, clutching a key.

As he fitted it into the lock, Lassiter turned on Freddie Peal. "If Pryor's done something to Elnora, you'll wish to hell I'd let them hang you!"

But they found Elnora, not dead but bound and gagged.

"He . . . he was coming back for me," she gasped, rubbing at the raw places at mouth corners made by the gag.

Lassiter's arm was rebandaged. Ryerson's body rested on a counter in the store. Peal had been locked in a shed.

By now, Elnora had heard the whole story. Neither she nor Lassiter, for that matter, could see how they managed to come out of it alive.

"A final brave act of his life," Elnora said to Maggie, speaking of her father grabbing the rifle that Pryor had made him drop.

Juanito, bandaged, his lacerations treated with arnica, looked at Elnora. "I guess it's up to me to help you run Aleman's Barn."

But it was Maggie who said, "She's perfectly capable of running it herself, Juanito. We need you at XR . . . as my partner." Her voice broke. "A cattle ranch to leave our kids . . ."

"One thing I don't understand," Elnora said. "What happened to the ransom money."

Lassiter managed a grunt of pain as he shifted his bandaged right arm and walked over to stare out a window at the litter of junk in the rear yard.

"The money . . . it just seemed to disappear," Maggie said. "If there really was any money. Nobody is sure."

Then she walked over and stood beside Lassiter, saying softly, "I know what happened, Lassiter. You earned every penny of it. Juanito agrees."

He turned and looked down at her, at the swollen cheek, the eyes reddened from a belated display of grief for her father. "I don't know what the hell you're talking about," he managed. At the time he wondered if they realized why he tarried at Tejano Lake after shouting at them to move out while he made a final search of the camp. "I'll catch up!" he had yelled at them.

"No money can buy human life," Maggie said, still in that soft voice. "We owe you ours."

He knew it wouldn't be an easy life for either of them; they both had much to learn. But given time . . .

"You're Juanito's blood brother," Maggie said with a shaky smile. "So that makes you mine."

She stood on tiptoe and kissed his cheek. He only shrugged.

Elnora fixed them a meal. "You'll need time for that wound to heal, Lassiter." She met his eyes across the table. He knew he'd stay around until he felt the urge to push on. One day he'd slip back to Tejano Lake and retrieve the satchel of money four feet down in the water at the end of a saddle rope tied to a submerged rock.

When a sound of horsemen was heard, Juanito limped to a window. "All we don't need now," he said in a shaking voice, peering out into the twilight, "is Sheriff Lambert and a posse."

Lassiter got up from the table, feeling the pain in his arm. "Let me do the talking," he said. "Our day is over. Lambert's is just starting." He looked around at the handsome widow Aleman and wanted to add, It's also starting for us. Especially the night . . .

Her shining eyes seemed to agree.

"Conley is among the most productive
and inventive of modern Western novelists."
—Dale L. Walker, *Rocky Mountain News*

BARJACK AND THE UNWELCOME GHOST

Marshal Barjack likes to keep peace and quiet in the tiny town of Asininity. It's better for business at the Hooch House, the saloon that Barjack owns. But peace and quiet got mighty hard to come by once Harm Cody came to town. Cody's made a lot of enemies over the years and some of them are hot on his trail, aiming to kill him—including a Cherokee named Miller and a pretty little sharpshooter named Polly Pistol. And when the Asininity bank gets robbed, well, now Cody has a whole new bunch of enemies . . . including Barjack.

Robert J. Conley

"One of the most underrated and overlooked writers
of our time, as well as the most skilled."
—Don Coldsmith, Author of the Spanish Bit Saga

ISBN 13: 978-0-8439-6225-3

The Classic Film Collection

The Searchers by Alan LeMay

Hailed as one of the greatest American films, *The Searchers,* directed by John Ford and starring John Wayne, has had a direct influence on the works of Martin Scorsese, Steven Spielberg, and many others. Its gorgeous cinematic scope and deeply nuanced characters have proven timeless. And now available for the first time in decades is the powerful novel that inspired this iconic movie.

Destry Rides Again by Max Brand

Made in 1939, the Golden Year of Hollywood, *Destry Rides Again* helped launch Jimmy Stewart's career and made Marlene Dietrich an American icon. Now available for the first time in decades is the novel that inspired this much-loved movie.

The Man from Laramie by T. T. Flynn

In its original publication, *The Man from Laramie* had more than half a million copies in print. Shortly thereafter, it became one of the most recognized of the Anthony Mann/ Jimmy Stewart collaborations, known for darker films with morally complex characters. Now the novel upon which this classic movie was based is once again available—for the first time in more than fifty years.

The Unforgiven by Alan LeMay

In this epic American novel, which served as the basis for the classic film directed by John Huston and starring Burt Lancaster and Audrey Hepburn, a family is torn apart when an old enemy starts a vicious rumor that sets the range aflame. Don't miss the powerful novel that inspired the film the *Motion Picture Herald* calls "an absorbing and compelling drama of epic proportions."
